The Pretend Detective

The Max Moran Fireside Inn Mysteries, Volume 1

Glen Ebisch

Published by As You Like It Press, 2022.

THE PRETEND DETECTIVE

First edition. March 14, 2022.

Written by Glen Ebisch.

Chapter One

I was standing at the registration desk at the Fireside Inn looking over the reservations for the next week when I heard the scream. I knew immediately that it had come from the third floor where Sarah (who now wanted to be called Gabriella) Levine was cleaning the rooms. Gabriella, as she adamantly wished to be called, had discovered, as a result of one of those do-it-yourself test kits, that she was only 90 percent Jewish and the remaining 10 percent was Spanish. Determined to get in touch with her Hispanic roots, she had asked us all to refer to her now as Gabriella and had taken to speaking her own unique version of Spanish accented English with the occasional real Spanish word thrown into the mix at random. That Gabriella knew virtually no Spanish meant she tended to speak a hodgepodge that was generally incomprehensible to speakers of either language and made Spanglish sound like high Castilian.

Even her scream had a weird Spanish lilt, which is how I knew it was Gabriella who was in distress. I was thinking all of this as I bolted up the steps to the third floor, arriving there breathless and worried. At first I saw nothing amiss, but a second accented scream sent me charging down the hall to a partially closed door. I slowly pushed the door open, wary about what I was going to encounter behind it.

Gabriella was standing in the center of the room, mop in hand, staring at the bed on which a man was lying. She looked at me as I entered the room and pointed at the figure with a dramatically extended arm, like a bad actress in a cheesy soap or an opera singer.

"*Esta muerto*," she announced in a shaky voice.

I had even less Spanish than Gabriella, but there was no need for a translation. The man on the bed was staring at the ceiling with unblinking eyes. He was dead in any language.

"What happened here?" I asked.

"*El hombre—*"

"In English, please, Sarah."

She looked around her as if there was someone else in the room.

"Whom are you addressing?" she asked in perfect English, if you ignored her Jersey accent.

I ran a hand over my forehead, feeling a headache coming on. "Sorry, Gabriella. Just tell me what you found when you entered the room."

"*Señor* Jenkins was lying on the bed just like that. I had knocked, and when he didn't answer, I used my passkey, and this is what I found." She waved her hands up and down as if showing an item on display and hoping I would purchase it.

"Had he complained of being ill?"

She gave a shrug that was more Gallic than Spanish, obviously washing her hands of the whole matter.

"Not as far as I know."

I took a quick survey of the room. A suitcase stood on the luggage rack at the foot of the bed. There was a pile of dirty clothes in one corner, and a sport coat had been thrown over a straight-backed chair. Nothing seemed to distinguish it from any other room currently being used at the inn, aside, of course, from the dead body on display in the center of it.

I forced myself to study the body objectively. He was a rather overweight man in his late fifties. Although he looked pale at the moment—understandable given the circumstances—I had seen him in the lobby several times and noted that he had been very florid. He had also once complained to me about how exhausting it was to walk up the two flights of stairs to his room, as if the absence of an elevator wasn't common in a bed and breakfast (B&B). I also remembered that he had been rather irate when I told him that he definitely could not smoke in his room, even if he opened a window. All in all, he had been a prime candidate for sudden death due to a heart attack or stroke.

I took some consolation in that fact, hoping that the police when called would quickly arrive at the same conclusion. People died all the time in hotels and inns, and it was only commented upon when the death was not due to natural causes.

"Can I get back to work now? I'm already running behind, and I get off at noon?" Gabriella asked.

"Yes. Leave this room as it is and go on to the next," I said. Suddenly, the pile of dirty clothes in the corner of the room began to move. Leaping to the conclusion that it must mean the presence of the creature dreaded the most by the providers of public accommodations, I frantically shouted, "Rat!" while darting to the other side of the room and futilely attempting to scramble up the wall.

I must point out that while such an action would prove embarrassing to any male, when you are six feet three and two hundred and twenty pounds of muscle with the chiseled jaw of a man's man, it is especially humiliating.

Gabriella, who had held her position, calmly said, "It is *Dinamita*."

"The rat has a name? What is it, your *pet*?" I asked sharply, moving away from the wall as anger replaced my feelings of humiliation.

"It's a dog, and it was Mr. Jenkins's pet."

"You mean Jenkins gave his dog a Spanish name?" I asked, thoroughly confused.

"Of course not. That is my name for him. His English name is Dynamite."

As the pile of clothes gradually fell away, I could see that it was definitely a small dog with rather long fur.

"You knew Jenkins was keeping a dog in his room?" I asked accusingly.

She nodded unfazed.

"Why didn't you report it to me?"

"Because he paid me not to."

Of course, the question hardly required asking. I could have fired Gabriella on the spot, but even bad staff is hard to find.

Dynamite came across the room and sniffed at the hem of my pants. He looked up at me with chocolate brown eyes. He appeared sad, as if he knew that he had lost his master.

"Does he bite?" I asked.

Gabriella snorted. "He hardly even barks. Mr. Jenkins would carry him around in a canvas bag most of the time and let him out for a walk when he needed to go. Dynamite is no trouble."

I reached down and gave him a tentative pat on the head, expecting at any moment to lose a hand to sharp little teeth, but Dynamite licked my fingers and his fur felt silky smooth. A sense of calmness came over me.

"He's a Chihuahua," Gabriella explained. "That's why I gave him a Spanish name."

"He doesn't look or act like one." My stereotype had always been of a rat-like creature that yapped incessantly.

"He's a long-haired Chihuahua. Mr. Jenkins said that he was a pure-bred and came from a very reputable breeder. That's why he has such a calm disposition."

"Then why did he name him Dynamite?" I asked.

I received another Gallic shrug.

"Well, why don't you continue with your work? I'll call the police. They'll probably want to speak to you."

For the first time, Gabriella looked uncomfortable.

"They won't have to check into my background, will they?" she asked.

"Why? What do you have to hide?"

She made a weak effort at an ingratiating smile. It wasn't her strong point. "Just a few youthful indiscretions. You know, stuff from way in the past."

Since she was only twenty-one, I thought her grasp of what constituted the past was somewhat foreshortened.

"I don't see why they would," I reassured her, while promising myself that I was definitely going to delve into her history more thoroughly myself.

I closed and locked the door to Mr. Jenkins's room as Gabriella returned to her cleaning.

"Don't tell the other guests that you found a body," I warned her.

She nodded. "*Mis labios están sellandos.*"

I didn't know what that meant, but I was too tired to ask.

Dynamite followed me down the stairs to the lobby. I took a cushion off a wing chair and put it on the floor to one side of the large fireplace that gave the inn its name. I pointed to it. Much to my surprise, Dynamite obediently walked over and curled up on the cushion facing toward the door, his eyes alertly surveying the lobby.

I smiled to myself. At least something in my environment obeyed me.

Chapter Two

The next day, I rolled out of bed early because I heard whimpering in my room. It took me a moment to realize that it was coming from my houseguest, Dynamite, who was sleeping on another cushion, this one placed in a corner of my bedroom. I have a small apartment down a short hall behind the lobby so I can be on the premises in case of an emergency. Deciding that whimpering might be a sign that he wanted to go out, a thought which was confirmed by the fact that he was standing by the rear door of my apartment doing a hippity-hop dance, I quickly pulled on some clothes. Fortunately, the police who had come to the scene of Jenkins's death yesterday morning were so relieved that I was willing to take responsibility for the dog that they had allowed me to keep the bag of dried food, a few toys, and the leash that were discovered in the room. I now attached the leash to Dynamite's collar and went out the rear door into the garden behind the inn.

The inn was a large Victorian that had once been the home of a prosperous family in the town of Lighthouse Point at the southern end of the New Jersey shore. On a street filled with many grand Victorians, it was one of the most impressive, being situated on a corner, and he paid extra—he being my Uncle Edward who owned the inn—to keep the grounds and the gardens tidied within an inch of their lives. So I took a plastic bag with me to dispose of any gifts Dynamite might leave behind.

As I stood outside in the cool morning air of early May, I thought about yesterday's events with a sense of satisfaction. What could have been an awkward situation, finding the dead body of a guest in a room, had ended surprisingly well. The police had arrived and taken a perfunctory glance around. A medical person had declared Carl Jenkins officially deceased, and the body had been discreetly taken away, or at least as discreetly as possible given he had to be carried through the lobby in the middle of the morning. But that wasn't as bad as it sounds, since all the guests had finished their included breakfast and had gone out to do touristy things by the time he was bundled down the stairs and into the waiting van.

The police had told me that they would be in touch with his next of kin and would contact me as to the disposal of his personal effects. I watched Dynamite snuffle around among the hostas and realized that he was no doubt one of those effects. I wondered whether Jenkins had a relative who was devoted enough to the dog to want him. I was a bit surprised to feel a sense of sadness at the thought of surrendering Dynamite. I would never have actively decided to get a dog, but now that one had dropped into my life, I was reluctant to give it up.

I ruefully admitted to myself that this was often the way with me. I never decided much in life, but if life decided it for me, I was happy enough to go along with it. This had led to my having a number of unusual girlfriends. Although my looks indicated that I was a man of decisive action, in reality, I was the model of passive acceptance. If something happened, I went along with it until it stopped, and then I cheerfully accepted that as well, which seemed to infuriate some of those former girlfriends who seemed to expect me to beg them to stay. But I felt an unusual longing to keep Dynamite, perhaps because so far he was considerably less trouble than the humans who had wandered into my life.

An hour later, Dynamite and I had both eaten, done our business, and were back at our posts. I was behind the registration desk in the lobby, greeting the guests as they made their way to the dining room for the breakfast component of a B&B, and Dynamite was on his cushion in the lobby, where he attracted a number of pats on the head and comments about his being a good boy from those heading into breakfast. I began to think that he might prove to be a marketing boon as well as a satisfying companion.

I was glancing over the proofs of an advertisement I planned to put in a shoreside magazine when I became aware of someone on the other side of the counter. I glanced up and was startled to see an attractive African American woman like me in her late twenties studying my face as if it were a road map and she was lost. I can say without vanity that women often give me second and third glances because of my rugged, romance-cover face and well-muscled body, which somehow developed even though I have avoided physical exercise since my early youth. I was fortunate to have gotten my mother to cajole one of her cousins who is a physician into declaring that I had to be excused from gym because of non-existent asthma.

The woman in front of me was dressed in a stylish suit, so I didn't know she was a police officer until she waved her credentials in front of me and announced, "I'm Detective Sergeant Azure Blue."

I felt an insane desire to reply that we must be related because I was Cerulean Blue. Of course, I resisted, but a smile must have crossed my lips because her gaze narrowed.

"Do you think my name is funny?" she asked sharply. Clearly, I'd touched a sore spot.

"Not at all. I would never laugh at a name, given my own."

She glanced at the nameplate on the front desk.

"Your name is Max Moran?"

I nodded.

"What's so odd about that?"

I sighed. This was not a story I cared to relate to a woman I had just met.

"I have three older brothers that my father named. He let my mother name me, and he always thought that Max was well . . . a bit effeminate."

Detective Blue gave me a puzzled look. "I don't see it. What were your brothers named?"

"Ryker, Duke, and Cash."

She struggled not to smile. "I can sort of understand that by comparison your name is a bit less decisive. What's your father's name?"

"Leslie. He was overcompensating."

She grinned outright this time. "Still, Max isn't so bad. I don't see it as effeminate."

"Well, you have to understand that it was part of an entire package. My brothers went into the HVAC business with Dad right out of high school. They install furnaces and compressors all around the Perth Amboy area when they aren't sitting in a bar watching sports. I went to college, over the objections of my father. He only relented when I agreed to major in business, but unknown to him, I doubled majored in theater."

The detective rolled her eyes. "He must have hated that."

"He wouldn't let me live at home after school. I spent a few years in Manhattan looking for work as an actor, supported in secret by my mother, but I only got parts off Broadway—some of them way off Broadway. Eventually, she prevailed on her brother Edward to make me manager of this inn when he decided to move to Florida a year ago. There are a couple of community theaters in town, so I still get to keep my hand in as an actor."

"It must have been hard to give up your dream."

I shrugged. "I could see the playbill on the wall. They insisted on casting me as the romantic hero, but I always came across more as the helpful best friend. I didn't project enough male charisma, they said."

"More beta than alpha male?"

"More zeta."

"Ah. Are you in anything right now in town?"

"I have the role of the detective in *The Butler Did It!* It's a mystery opening next weekend in the theater in the basement of the Presbyterian Church. It's a pretty meaty part. I got it because there weren't any other men under sixty who tried out for the role."

"It's a mystery, you say?"

I nodded.

She leaned across the counter confidentially and asked, "So who committed the crime?"

I gave her a puzzled look. "The butler, of course."

She leaned back. "I never would have guessed that."

I nodded. "The playwright thought reverse psychology would leave the audience stunned."

"Hmm."

"And how did you get the name Azure?"

"My mother is a painter," she said shortly. The detective cleared her throat to indicate that the informal conversation was over. "You found the dead body of a Carl Jenkins in one of your rooms yesterday, I understand?"

I was about to reply when Gabriella breezed in the front door.

"*Hola*," she called out gaily.

"Actually, she found the body," I explained.

"Does she speak English or will I need a translator?" Azure asked in a whisper.

"Trust me. A translator wouldn't help. Anyway, I thought Mr. Jenkins's death was due to natural causes. What is there to ask about?"

"Yeah. His arteries were more clogged than the streets into town on a Saturday at the height of summer. That's what killed him for sure, but it turns out that he was a private investigator. He had his credentials on him. So I just wanted to tie up some loose ends and find out if he was here on vacation or working a case."

"I didn't know his profession." I turned to where Gabriella was about to go up the stairs. "Gabriella, do you have a minute to speak with the police?"

She spun around and turned pale. She began walking back toward us as if trying to decide whether to confess or make a break for the door. When she finally got within range, I introduced her to Detective Blue.

"Can you understand me?" the detective asked, pronouncing each word slowly and loudly.

"Of course I can," Gabriella replied in one of her unaccented moods. "I'm not deaf."

"Great. Did Mr. Jenkins tell you that he was a private detective?"

Gabriella nodded.

"Did he tell you whether he was in town working on a case?"

She nodded again, apparently having suddenly lost fluency in any language.

"Did he tell you what he was working on?" Blue asked.

Another nod.

"What was it?" the detective asked, her voice just below the level of a shout.

"He said he was looking for a missing girl."

"Did he tell you anything more than that?"

She shook her head. "But it must have been written down in his black book."

"What black book?" the detective and I asked simultaneously.

"The one he kept under his mattress."

"Why didn't you mention this before?" I asked.

Gabriella shrugged. "No preguntaste."

"What does that mean?" I snapped.

"It means 'You didn't ask,'" Detective Blue answered.

"You speak Spanish?"

She shook her head. "I just know that's always the excuse witnesses give when they withhold information."

Detective Blue and I bounded up the stairs to the third floor of the inn. Actually, she bounded, while I followed at a more sedate pace. When we reached Jenkins's former room, I unlocked the door, and we went inside. The detective walked around examining things. There wasn't much to see since a uniformed officer had removed all of Jenkins's effects yesterday.

Finally, she nodded. "Lift the mattress."

It took me a minute to realize that she intended that I do the physical labor. I braced myself, inserted my hands between the mattress and the box spring, and heaved. It rose up rather quickly since it was only a full-size bed. I heard her give a little grunt of triumph and reach under the mattress. Her hand came out holding a black book about the size of a diary. I felt a moment of sadness at the thought that the man who had written in that little book on a regular basis was now no more.

As I lowered the mattress, I heard Detective Blue give a muttered curse.

"What's the matter?" I asked.

She handed me the book. I opened it to the last page with writing on it. About half the page was full. It was one long paragraph with words written in apparently random order. At times, it flirted with making sense, but then, just as you started to get excited, quickly veered off into gibberish. I surmised that it was either written in code or a paragraph from Joyce's *Ulysses*.

"I hate it when people write things in code. Does an over-the-hill private eye really know anything that's important enough to hide from the rest of the world?" Blue complained.

"We'll never find out, unless you have a cryptographer down at the station that can decipher it."

She gave me a scornful look. "There are only ten of us. The chief handles the paperwork, two civilian women do dispatch, six officers patrol the town, and I handle all the criminal investigations. *Does it sound like we have a cryptographer on staff?*"

"I suppose not," I said meekly, taking a step back from the angry woman.

She brushed past me and headed down the stairs. I stopped to lock the door and thought she would be gone by the time I returned to the lobby. But she was standing by the registration desk looking contrite.

"Sorry about that hissy fit. Sometimes the job gets to me."

I smiled my forgiveness. "It must be a very frustrating job in the long run."

She nodded. "Well, thank you for all the help. At least I know more than I did before. If you learn anything else, please let me know."

I told her that I would. "Do you know if Jenkins had any next of kin? I was primarily thinking about the dog." Over by the fireplace, Dynamite looked up as if he knew he was being talked about.

"Apparently, he was alone in the world. I could have the dog taken to the pound if you don't want it."

"That's okay. We seem to be getting along well," I said quickly.

She smiled. "You're a softie."

"So I've been told." *Too many times to count*, I thought.

"And if I have the opportunity, I'll come and see you in *The Butler Did It!*"

"I'll get you a free ticket for opening night. That's this coming Saturday. At least you won't find the play frustrating because it's not like police work. You already know who did it."

"Yes, I guess there is that to feel good about," she replied with a sad smile.

Chapter Three

Carole Rawlins came out from the dining room and slipped in behind the desk. She worked as a waitress during breakfast and covered the registration desk in the afternoon. Divorced and in her midthirties, she had a small son and worked at the inn during the season as a way to augment whatever she had gotten from her divorce settlement. She was a sensible—if annoyingly acerbic—woman, but given her commanding nature, I thought my Uncle Edward would have been better advised to hire her to manage the inn than myself. I also knew this because she repeatedly told me. I was glad he hadn't, but I felt guilty at taking advantage of nepotism to get my position. I had promised myself that if I ever left this job, I would highly recommend her as my replacement.

"I'll take over at the desk for a while," she said. "I think you have to get to the kitchen. We have a bit of a situation there."

"A fire?" I asked, startled.

"Nothing that dire. But, apparently, one of the male guests has taken a liking to Mrs. Hazlet. He came into the kitchen after breakfast was over and complimented her on her waffles."

"That sounds innocent enough, unless waffles is some kind of a euphemism."

Carole frowned. "I don't think so."

I didn't think so either. Mrs. Hazlet was a sturdy woman in her fifties who flaunted her scones more than her charms. Although, I reminded myself not to underestimate her appeal because rumor had it that she and Uncle Edward had a long-standing relationship that was more than culinary. When I first arrived on the scene a year ago, she had threatened to quit because of my uncle's almost immediate departure to Florida in the darkness of night. But I had managed to prevail upon her to stay by pointing out that my uncle claimed that his relocation was only temporary. But a year later, Uncle Edward still remained vague in his emails about when or whether he planned to return to Lighthouse Point. But by now, Mrs. Hazlet seemed to have settled down and was no longer threatening to quit. I hoped a new admirer wouldn't stir up trouble.

"What do you want me to do about it?" I asked. Carole usually had an answer to everything.

"Well, I think you should go into the kitchen and see if Mrs. Hazlet is comfortable with having one of the guests sitting there chatting with her."

I frowned. "But how can I diplomatically ask a guest to leave the kitchen. I can't come on like a Victorian father and order him to stop sweet-talking my cook."

Carole gave me an exasperated look as if to suggest that she had to do everything.

"You could point out in a friendly way that Board of Health regulations restrict access to the kitchen to employees."

"Is that true?"

"I don't know, but neither will he."

I considered asking Carole to do it, but even I have a few limitations on my willingness to abandon my position of masculine command. I nodded and slowly walked out from behind the registration desk.

"Take over here," I ordered Carole, as if she was at the helm of a destroyer in the midst of an enemy flotilla.

I went through the dining room, admiring as I always did the floor-to-ceiling windows that lent a formal graciousness to the room. I pushed open the swinging door to the kitchen. I hoped that I wasn't disturbing a heated argument or a passionate embrace. I was only comfortable with demonstrative emotions on the stage.

A dapper man in his fifties was sitting casually at the counter that occupied the center of the room as if he belonged there. It was where Mrs. Hazlet did most of her preparation, and I knew she didn't like people perched there, looming over her work. I recognized the man to be Randolph Fuller, a fifty-something guest staying at the inn on his own. He was a slender, dapper-looking man in khakis and a knit shirt. I expected Mrs. Hazlet to be glaring at him, but she was nodding and coming as close to a smile as I'd seen since Uncle Edward left. Fuller was speaking.

"So it took me a long time to get accustomed to real maple syrup because I'd only had the phony stuff while I was a boy. When we're not accustomed to the best, we don't recognize it even when it slaps us in the face. Anyone who was raised on purchased bake goods would not be able to appreciate the muffins and breads you put out every day."

Mrs. Hazlet came as close to a girlish simper as I'd have thought possible.

"Thank you for that, but I'm not sure that anything I do is superior to what any good home cook could produce. It is just a matter of having been well trained by my mother and having had lots of experience."

"But I'm sure you add your own touch to everything you make."

"Well, I do try to make small improvements to every recipe I use."

He slapped the countertop. "That's the soul of creativity, making incremental changes in what experts have done before. Progress is the result of a series of many small steps."

Mrs. Hazlet gazed at him. "Now that you say it, I suppose that's true." She looked away from Fuller and saw me standing in the doorway. "Can I help you, Mr. Moran?"

"Umm. I just wanted to see if everything was all right." Unless I had read the situation very incorrectly, Mrs. Hazlet didn't need rescuing, so the threat of the health board would be inappropriate.

"Everything is fine," she reassured me.

"I assume you don't work in the evenings?" Fuller asked her.

"I get off at noon, once I've finished the preparations for the next day."

"Very good. Would you like to have dinner with me this evening? If you're free, that is? Perhaps you could recommend a restaurant in town.

Since I'm alone, it would be very nice to have a companion for dinner who is knowledgeable about food."

"That would be very nice," she replied.

I backed out the door, deciding that my intervention was neither needed nor wanted. I returned to the desk where Carole was working on the computer updating a program, no doubt, so I wouldn't be able to make sense of it without her help.

"Did you get him out of there?" she asked.

"I was too late. They were already arranging to have dinner together."

Carole gave me a withering glance and shook her head. "Don't you realize that if Mrs. Hazlet gets married again, she'll quit working here, and the only thing that makes the Fireside Inn special is the high quality of its breakfasts?"

I shrugged. "There wasn't anything I could do. The guy is pretty suave, and she was obviously enchanted with him."

"Is that what you're going to tell your Uncle Edward when he wants to know how you let his girlfriend slip through your fingers?"

"No, I'm going to tell him that if he wanted to keep her, he shouldn't have been skulking in Florida but should have been up here wooing the woman he loves."

"If Uncle Edward were here, you wouldn't be necessary," she reminded me.

I gave her my haughtiest expression; one that I'd perfected in the role of Oscar Wilde in a play at the *Highly Experimental Theatre Workshop* on Staten Island. I still remember the single critic from the suburbs who saw the play, writing, "No Oscar for Oscar." Critics can be cruel, especially the insignificant ones.

"No, I would be the assistant manager, and you wouldn't be necessary," I said, looking so far down my nose at her that I went cross-eyed.

She laughed. "Oh, really. You think Edward would keep you and fire me."

"Of course," I said, with more certainty than I felt. "Blood is thicker than water."

"Well, blood may be thicker than water, Max, but you're lite beer and I'm Napoleon brandy. Which do you think your uncle would prefer to drink?"

The leap in metaphors left me stunned for a moment.

"I think he prefers scotch."

Carole gave a huff and marched out of the lobby, leaving me in blessed peace.

I thought she might be right, and that Uncle Edward would happily replace me. He was an extremely wealthy man in his fifties who had made a lot of money in a series of start-up companies that he had created and sold for many millions. He didn't have any creative ideas himself, but he could recognize them and get other people to invest. I wasn't sure how much patience he would have with someone like me who was content to stand behind a desk and watch the world go by. As long as he stayed in Florida, I wouldn't have to find out.

Chapter Four

The day wore on slowly, as days usually do in the hotelier trade. Calls came in and reservations were booked. Beds were changed, rooms cleaned, and guests made to feel special. I took Dynamite out for a couple of brief walks to relieve the monotony of the day and explained carefully to him all the challenges of my chosen career. He looked up, with his tongue hanging out and a rapt expression on his face, as if he understood all and sympathized. I suspected that he was the only one who did.

Right after lunch, I was about to turn the desk over to Carole, who was just finishing up setting the tables in the dining room for tomorrow's breakfast, when a woman in her midthirties walked into the lobby, took off her sunglasses with a dramatic flourish, and marched up to the desk. She was wearing a stylishly tailored blouse and shorts that revealed a pair of long, slim muscular legs. She had black hair and green eyes, which were focused on me. She smiled in a way that was both beguiling and intimidating.

"I hope you can help me," she said, putting her nicely manicured hands on the desk.

I certainly hope so, I thought but didn't say. Instead, I just gave her my polite innkeeper's smile.

"I'd like to contact one of your guests, a Mr. Carl Jenkins."

You'll need a Ouija board, I responded in my mind.

"I'm afraid that isn't possible," I replied with a sad expression.

"He's living somewhere else?"

That was an interesting theological discussion that I didn't want to have.

"I'm afraid Mr. Jenkins passed away yesterday."

A shocked expression came over her face.

"That's terrible. He was working for me. He called two days ago and said I should come down here because he had some information for me."

"You employed him as a private detective?"

Her eyes narrowed.

"You knew his profession?"

"Not until after his death. The police found his credentials among his effects."

"How did he die?"

"The police believe it was a heart attack."

She stared across the lobby with a thoughtful expression. "Since the police apparently confided in you, did they have any information about the case he was working on for me?"

"They found his notebook, but he wrote everything in code. So, as far as I know, no one knows anything about his last case."

"Then there's no way for me to find out why he wanted to see me." She gave a deep sigh, and her eyes filled with tears.

"Was it something very important to you that he was working on?" I asked.

She nodded. "He was trying to find my younger sister who disappeared three weeks ago. She was working for a company in Brooklyn and just suddenly took off. She said something about heading for the Jersey Shore and going as far south as she could. That's all her roommate was able to tell me."

"Why did she run off?"

"We're not sure. She never told us very much about her life once she moved to the city after she graduated from college." She suddenly put her hand out across the desk. "Excuse me for not introducing myself. I'm Brianna McCall. My sister is Rachel McCall."

I took her hand, which gripped mine strongly.

"Didn't her roommate know why she left town?"

"Well, she did say that Rachel had recently broken things off with her long-time boyfriend."

"Moving from Brooklyn to South Jersey seems like a bit of an overreaction," I said.

Brianna smiled. "My sister was always the emotional one in the family. When something doesn't go right for her, she turns it into a three-act drama. But I was surprised that she left her job without telling anyone. From what her roommate said, I was starting to wonder whether she'd had some kind of a breakdown. Mom and Dad have both retired to Florida, so I was nominated to find out what's happened to her."

"And you hired Jenkins to look into it for you?"

"I had no idea how to begin to find a missing person. I didn't want to involve the police until I had more information about what might have happened to Rachel. Mr. Jenkins came highly recommended, and he knew the area."

"Did he give you any idea what he had found out?"

"He said that he knew she was living in Lighthouse Point, but he wouldn't tell me any more over the phone." Brianna frowned. "I think he wanted another payment before giving me more information. Now that he's dead, I'm really stuck."

"Well, if you know that she's living in Lighthouse Point, it might be time to go to the police."

Brianna inclined her head closer to mine until I could catch the floral aroma of her perfume.

"The thing is, Rachel has a history of drug problems. That's the reason the family is so worried about her. She seemed to have finally gotten straightened out after some ups and downs during college. We were hoping that once she was older and had a steady job she would settle down and go along on an even keel. But if she's become involved with drugs again, I wouldn't want to get her into trouble with the police."

I admitted that I understood why that might be the case.

She gave me a speculative once over. "You look like a guy who can take care of himself."

I cringed. Some of the worst experiences in my life have started with those words.

"Well . . ." I couldn't quite find the words to tell an attractive woman that my looks could be deceiving.

"You probably know this area pretty well, don't you?"

"I guess I do," I admitted.

"Well, I was wondering if you could do a little looking around for me. You would know who to talk to and where to look far better than I would. People might find you more . . . intimidating . . . than they would find me."

If they didn't know me, maybe, I thought.

"And I know your time is valuable. I'd be happy to pay you the same fifty dollars an hour that Jenkins was getting. Just keep a record of your hours and any expenses, and I'll cover them."

I paused, trying to think of a way to tell her that I really wasn't the man for the job because I wasn't the man I appeared to be.

She leaned forward again and gave me a tremulous smile. "I need help finding Rachel before anything bad happens to her. Will you help me?"

What could I do? I said what she wanted to hear.

Chapter Five

Armed with a photograph of Rachel I'd been given by Brianna, I set out on my mission as soon as Carole took over the desk for me. She asked where I was going. I said that I thought I'd take a walk around town with Dynamite. That appeared to startle her, since I wasn't exactly known for engaging in any unnecessary physical exercise. Normally, I spent the afternoons in my apartment reading a book or doing idle research on the computer. But today I had a purpose in mind. Brianna had given me her cell phone number and asked me to call her this evening to report on my findings, so I had to get started right away in order to have something to report.

Before I even reached the front door, however, I realized that wandering around Lighthouse Point going to every B&B and hotel was not the smart way to do this. It would waste time and be exhausting. Jenkins hadn't become portly by doing a lot of legwork. A smart detective would use the phone or computer as the way to gather information. I didn't want to give Carole the satisfaction of seeing me turn around in the lobby and head back to my apartment, so I continued out the front door and scooted around the corner

and through the back garden. Dynamite looked up at me in puzzlement as we walked in a circle but said nothing, proving that he truly was man's best friend.

Being an innkeeper, I had on my computer a list of all the hotels, motels, and B&Bs in Lighthouse Point Armed with their phone numbers, I could easily call each with my inquiry. My finger was all set to push the buttons of the first number when I realized that no one was going to tell me anything unless I had a good cover story in place, a.k.a. a convincing lie. Even though I was a fellow hotelier, that would not be enough for them to violate confidentiality unless I made it more palatable for them. After some thought, I decided to claim that I was Rachel's brother, and I was trying to reach her because our father had been taken desperately ill. I decided that my acting chops would make this successful. I even sat for a few minutes—like I'd been taught in method acting—to get into a distressed frame of mind, picturing our poor bedridden father in the hospital feebly asking to see Rachel. It brought tears to my eyes.

My record was mixed, just as my acting career had been so far. Of the first ten places I called, three categorically refused to give me any information about their guests. The other seven were happy to spill the beans, but had no record of the woman as a guest or on their staff. It was on lucky eleven that I hit pay dirt.

The woman at the Gray Gull Inn listened to my tale of woe, making all the appropriate commiserating sounds, and she informed me that they did indeed have a Rachel McCall on their staff as a waitress. She was due to come in for the dinner shift at four o'clock. The nice woman even volunteered to call Rachel to break the bad news, but I insisted that I wanted to do it in person. She did, however, draw the line at giving me Rachel's address or phone number, so I was going to have to meet Rachel at the Gray Gull to tell her about Dad.

I debated the idea of simply giving Brianna the information and having her make the contact with her sister, but after all the effort I had already expended, I wanted to carry out the job to its conclusion. I was pretty sure that if I talked with her, I could convince Rachel to meet with her loving sister who had traveled all this way to see her.

In any event, at quarter to four I was standing outside the Gray Gull Inn. To the casual observer, I was a six-foot-three guy walking a Chihuahua up and down the same block, as if he had nothing better in life to do other than wait for his dog to poop. Actually, I had to be back at the reception desk by four-thirty to relieve Carole or else endure another lecture on how she could do my job far better than I. She might be right, but I was thoroughly tired on having my nose rubbed in it.

Fortunately, right at five to four I saw a young woman wearing a waitress's outfit coming up the street toward me. I took what I hoped was a surreptitious glance at the photo I pulled out of my pocket to confirm that this was indeed Rachel McCall. She was tall and willowy and coming toward me with a rapid stride. I stepped in front of her at the last minute.

"Excuse me, are you Rachel McCall?" I asked.

She hit me with a right hook that would have done serious damage if I hadn't moved my head backward at the last second. But it still brought tears to my eyes. She tried to turn and run, but I managed to step forward and seize her arm with my left hand, since my right was gripping Dynamite's leash.

"Let me explain . . ." I managed to say as she tried to pull away from me.

I held on to her arm for dear life, hoping that there were no onlookers in the act of calling the police. Finally, she gave up trying to break away and started pummeling me again as I moved my head back and forth, dodging her blows like a maniacal bobblehead. Deciding that it was only a matter of time before she landed a solid shot, I dropped Dynamites leash in an attempt to protect my face with my right hand.

I'm not sure how long this contest would have continued, probably until the nearest patrol car pulled up and the cops bundled me into the back seat. But suddenly there was the deep rumble of a wild animal growling, and in a flurry of teeth and fur, Dynamite charged into the fray, pulling fiercely on Rachel's pants leg. Although he was obviously taking on a bigger job than he was suited for, there was something intimidating in the fury with which he approached his task. Rachel stopped hitting me, and for the first time I saw fear in her eyes as she tried to pull away from Dynamite.

I reached down, grabbed the dog's leash from the sidewalk and gave it a firm pull.

"No, Dynamite! No!"

He immediately disengaged from his attack and came to stand by my side looking up as if asking for further orders. Rachel seemed as surprised as I was at the speed with which he had transformed from a fiend from hell into a docile little dog.

Rachel gave me a quizzical look.

"I don't know," I said. "I just got him . . . from a dead man."

Her eyes narrowed, and I was afraid she might begin hitting me again.

"Look, I'm sorry if I frightened you, but I have a message for you from your sister. She asked me to find you."

Her eyes narrowed even more into a gunfighter's squint.

"I don't have a sister," she said.

"You don't?" It was my turn to be surprised. "Hmm. There's a woman who says she's your sister who asked me to find you."

"Is she here now?" Rachel asked, glancing around nervously.

"I don't think so," I replied, surveying the scene for myself and not spotting anyone.

"What did she tell you?" the woman asked, and then she glanced at her watch. "Look, I can't talk now. I have to get to work or I'll lose my job. Can we meet after work? I get out right after nine."

"Okay. Where do you want to meet?"

"How about at the Busted Beacon at nine-thirty," she replied, naming a popular bar in the center of the pedestrian mall.

I agreed.

"Don't tell this woman that you've found me. Will you do that?"

"Not until we've had a chance to talk," I promised.

She gave me what might have been a faint smile before turning and heading into the inn.

"What do you make of that Dynamite?" I asked, watching her leave.

He gave what probably passed for a doggy shrug.

Chapter Six

"Act like you've got a pair, Max. Stop raising your voice at the end of an accusation so it comes out like a question. You sound like some ditzy Valley girl. When you're accusing someone of murder, convince us that you mean it," Mrs. Federico shouted at me.

Mrs. Federico was a sweet-looking grandmotherly type who often got the role of the . . . well . . . sweet grandmother in local productions. But when she was working as director, as she was with *The Butler Did It!* all of that sweetness disappeared to be replaced by a stern-faced dominatrix. And that was the Mrs. Federico who was staring at me right now. I expected her to reach for a whip at any moment.

"Sorry," I mumbled.

She sighed with exasperation, and then snapped, "Don't be sorry, Max, just get it right."

Gerald Simmons, who played the major, and his wife Gloria Simmons, who played his wife in the production and also in real life, looked on with blank expressions. They ran a small bed and breakfast a few blocks from mine. They were frequently cast as the lord and lady of the manor because they had an aristocratic look about them, even though they originally came from Jersey City. Their great strength was the ability to always look bored, which was true in real life as well as onstage.

Chelsea Dowell, who played their pretty blonde daughter—but not in real life—gave me a sympathetic smile. She had made clear her interest in me early on in rehearsals. Even though I had tried to suggest to her that I was not the man of action that I appeared, she refused to be discouraged. Even Mrs. Federico's repeated suggestions that I was lacking in the testicular department didn't seem to faze her.

Rick Owens, the manager of the local hardware store who played the butler/murderer, smirked at me. Partly this was because a smirk was the expression he usually presented to the world, and partly it was jealousy due the fact that he had designs on Chelsea, but she only had eyes for me.

"Now accuse Rick of being a murderer like you mean it," Mrs. Federico demanded.

The scene called for me to walk up to Rick, poke my finger into his chest, and say with a dramatic flourish, "I know that you are the murderer!"

As I walked toward him, he whispered, "Yeah, Max, at least try to pretend to be a man."

I took a long step forward and jammed my stiff index finger hard into his chest. "You are the murderer!" I shouted, as Rick reeled backward, clutching his chest as if in cardiac arrest.

"What the hell are you trying to do? Kill me," Rick bellowed, after he regained his breath. "That's supposed to be a poke, not an attempt to puncture my lung."

"Suck it up, Rick," Mrs. Federico said, shoving a wave of blue-gray hair from her forehead. "I like it. We'll keep it. That adds dramatic tension."

Rick frowned. He opened his mouth to speak but changed his mind, as Mrs. Federico cowed even him with her hard, directorial stare. I gazed down at the ground, a bit ashamed that I had given in to his juvenile taunting with violence.

We rehearsed the scene a few more times, with my poke in Rick's chest being somewhat more moderated, until Mrs. Federico declared that it was time to wrap it up for the night. I hurried toward the door. I had been surreptitiously studying my watch for the last ten minutes. It was getting close to nine-thirty and the church that served as our theater was three blocks away from the Busted Beacon.

I felt a small hand on my arm as I reached the exit. I turned and Chelsea gave me a shy smile. "Would you have time to go out for a drink, Max?"

"Sorry, Chelsea, I have to get back to the inn. Lexi, the college student covering the desk for me, has to leave at ten." That was true, but not my real reason for stiffing Chelsea.

She nodded and gave me a bright, heroic smile that broke my heart. "Some other time, then."

I nodded and grinned. "Sure," I said, although I thought she could do better than me.

As I left, I saw Rick moving in on Chelsea. I was sorry to see that. If she could do better than me, she could certainly do better than Rick.

I half walked and half jogged from the church to the Busted Beacon. The bar was moderately crowded for a weekday. May is still early in the season, so it was a mix of regulars and a few tourists getting a jump on the summer. I stood in the entrance and scanned the crowd looking for Rachel. I wondered if she had been delayed or given up on me because I was ten minutes late. As I walked further inside, I spotted her in the far back corner near the doors to the kitchen. She was wearing a gray hoodie with the hood pulled up. It may have disguised her identity, but it made her as conspicuous as a bank robber stopping off for a beer between jobs.

I approached the table. "Is this seat taken?" I asked, trying for casual humor.

"Were you followed?"

"I don't think so."

"Did you look?"

"Sort of."

She snorted and waved a hand, which I took as an indication that I should sit down. She had a beer in front of her, and when the waitress hurried over, I ordered the same. The Busted Beacon was known for its wide variety of beers. Regular patrons even had their own personal beer mugs lined up on a shelf across the room. When one of them died, the mug would be turned around to face west—a fitting, if somewhat morbid tribute, to a serious drinker.

"I don't know if I can trust you," Rachel said.

Every conversation I've ever had with a woman that began that way has always ended up with me in trouble, so I gave a cautious answer.

"Hmm. That all depends on what you want me to do." I noticed that Rachel was rather attractive by the dim glow of the bar lights.

"I'm not asking you *to do* anything. *I'm* asking you *not to do* something."

"Okay." I frowned. I had never been much good at puzzles. "What *don't* you want me to do?"

"*Don't* tell this woman who hired you that you've found me."

"You mean *don't* tell Brianna McCall, your sister?"

"I *don't have* a sister. I told you that."

"Then *who* is this woman who is looking for you?" I asked, getting really tired of this emphatic conversation.

She sighed and took a sip of her beer. "I have no idea."

"Well, why is she looking for you?"

"If I told you that, it would put your life in danger."

I had taken a sip of my beer but suddenly found it difficult to swallow.

"Uh, maybe it would be better if you didn't tell me then."

She shrugged. "Probably it's already too late."

I didn't like the sound of that.

"What do you mean?"

"This person looking for me isn't going to believe you, no matter what you say. I was hoping that if I kept quiet and left town, they'd leave me alone, but I guess I was wrong."

"Why are these people looking for you?"

Before Rachel could answer, I saw Brianna McCall walk into the bar. She was wearing a black sweater and jeans, looking really hot in a cat burglar sort of way. She paused in the doorway to survey the room. Fortunately, our corner was invisible from the doorway, but that would only last a moment.

"Brianna is here," I hissed.

"She must have followed you," Rachel said with an accusing look.

"Maybe not. She might just be prowling the bars looking for you."

"I doubt it."

"Do you want to argue the point some more?" I asked. "Or should we get out of here?"

She jumped up, heading for the front door. I grabbed her arm and began dragging her toward the kitchen. "This way," I ordered.

We charged through the swinging doors, almost knocking over a waitress carrying a tray piled high with food.

"Sorry," I mumbled, as we rushed past the startled kitchen staff and out through the back door.

We ran across the rear parking lot and paused under a tree that just might conceal us. I looked back to see if we were being followed. I waited what seemed like several minutes but was probably only a few seconds. I could feel the sweat drying on my body in the cool breeze of the early May evening. It was the sweat of both exertion and fear.

"You have to tell me what this is all about," I said, turning to Rachel.

There was no one there. I was staring at an empty parking lot. She had quietly run off into the darkness, leaving me to wonder what I had gotten myself into.

I just hoped that whatever it was, it wouldn't get my beer mug turned to the west.

Chapter Seven

I returned to the inn, walking as fast as I could while jumping at shadows, imagining that each one was someone with a knife or gun intent on doing me in. I finally walked into the lobby at ten-twenty suffering from nervous exhaustion. Lexi was standing behind the desk or rather hiding behind it. I could just make out the top of her head where she was sitting reading a book. Lexi was a shy young woman who for some reason had chosen to major in communications in the hopes of someday being a television anchorperson. I had the feeling that this was a job for a person with a more assertive personality, but I didn't want to disillusion her. Although I certainly could have, based on my personal experience. Know thyself might be a good motto, but it was a lot easier said than done.

"You're back early, Mr. Moran" Lexi said in a loud whisper, jumping to her feet. She always spoke rather softly in an effort to go unnoticed. For the longest time, I had worried that I was going deaf.

"Yes . . . well . . . things didn't go exactly as planned." I took out my wallet and handed her what I owed. "You can go along home now."

She stared at the money. "But this is what we agreed upon for me staying until eleven." She glanced over at the grandfather clock. "I still have twenty-five more minutes."

"So you do," I said, giving her a benevolent smile. "Consider the difference a tip."

For a moment I thought she was going to argue the toss, but then she gave a diffident nod. She packed up her books and left with a soft goodbye. I stood behind the desk and watched her leave, trying to decide what I was going to tell Brianna. She had specifically asked me to phone her with a report tonight, and I was struggling to decide what to tell her. I don't like to lie, but apparently Brianna had lied first by misrepresenting herself as Rachel's sister. If someone lies to you first, is it then okay to lie to her in return. But what if it was Rachel who was lying to me, and Brianna really was her sister. My head began to hurt.

One thing was certain; I had to contact Brianna with some kind of report. It was almost eleven, but I suspected that Brianna was still out prowling the bars in the hunt for Rachel, and if she didn't hear from me, I might well find her knocking on the door of the inn. I reluctantly made the call.

"Hello, Max, it's good to hear from you," Brianna said, making it sound like she had expected to be contacted sooner.

"Yes . . . well . . . it's been kind of busy. However, I was able to secure a list of all the places one can stay in Lighthouse Point, and I've been calling everyone on the list."

"Any luck?"

The moment of truth or untruth had arrived. I took a deep breath.

"Not so far. I've only made it about a third of the way through the list. I hope to do another third by tomorrow, and I should be able to complete it by the next day."

"I was hoping for faster results," Brianna said in a cool voice. "You do realize that this is a troubled young woman out there all by herself. We don't know what her mental condition might be, so it's imperative we get in touch with her as soon as possible."

"Right. Well, I might be able to find some extra time tomorrow morning to put into the calls. I'll try to complete the list by then."

"Very good, Max. I'll stop by the inn at noon to get your report and pay what I owe you so far."

"Okay," I replied. Not anxious to see Brianna face-to-face so soon, but unable to think of a convincing excuse.

"Fine. See you then," she said, somehow making it sound like a threat.

I called Dynamite over from his cushion in the lobby and put the leash on him. We walked up and down the block in front of the inn as Dynamite did his business and I worried about mine. I had a sinking feeling that by agreeing to become Brianna's eyes and ears, I had gotten into something way over my head. And now, by agreeing with Rachel to lie to Brianna, I had gotten even deeper in the quagmire. I wasn't sure how I was going to get out of all this. My Uncle Edward frequently said that when things seem most hopeless, it's best to get a good night's sleep because problems always appeared more solvable in the morning. If he had followed his own advice, maybe he wouldn't have run off to Florida in the middle of the night.

I hoped he was right.

*****

The next morning, I was standing behind the reservations desk with no more idea of what I was going to do than I'd had the night before. I suppose I could have continued going down my list, searching for where Rachel might be staying, but I didn't want to know. If I did know where Rachel was living, I'd be tempted, under pressure, to tell Brianna. I really didn't want to do that. Of course, knowing where she was living would help me contact Rachel. I knew that I needed to speak with her again to find out why she was on the run so I'd at least be aware of what I'd gotten involved in. But right now, I had no way of contacting her except to waylay her outside the Gray Gull Inn at four o'clock. Paralyzed by indecision, I spent all morning stewing about how I was going to lie convincingly to Brianna, who struck me as someone who was not going to be easy to fool.

After the breakfast rush, Carole came out of the dining room and stood next to me behind the desk. Since Carole didn't spend any more time around me than was absolutely necessary, I knew there was something she wanted to complain about, something that would be a further indication that she should be the manager rather than myself.

"Mrs. Hazlet is starry-eyed. I guess her date with Randolph Fuller went well."

"That's nice," I said, pretending to be busy with the day's mail.

"He's back in the kitchen again, making himself at home. Apparently, he's a widower with what amounts to a mansion in Westchester County, New York, and I overheard him telling her about how he likes to travel to Europe at least once a year."

"Sounds like fun."

"Don't you see?" Carole said, grabbing my arm and spinning me to face her. She was much stronger than she looked, being filled with the righteous anger of one who knows she should have my job.

"See what?" I said, giving Carole my best pleasantly blank expression.

"He's seducing her. Before we know it, we'll be without a fine cook, and your Uncle Edward will be without a girlfriend."

I sighed. "First of all, as you say, Mrs. Hazlet is a fine cook, but we can always recruit another who is almost as good. I'm not willing to stand in the way of her happiness just so I can enjoy her fluffy pancakes every morning. Secondly, Uncle Edward is the one who ran off and left Mrs. Hazlet almost a year ago. Even he must realize that no woman is going to wait around indefinitely for him. I'm not sure my uncle deserves her."

"But shouldn't we notify him that she has a suitor?"

"Why? So he can return, win her back, and then disappear again, leaving her heart broken. I don't think she deserves that."

Carole paused. I could see she was marshaling a further argument.

"There's something about this Fuller guy that just doesn't ring true. I mean, Mrs. Hazlet isn't exactly a beauty. Why is he acting so enamored?"

"As men get older, they find things other than physical beauty attractive. Mrs. Hazlet would be a fine homemaker, and she has a very pleasant personality." Unlike you, I wanted to add, but I didn't want to hurt her feelings because then Carole would hurt me physically. Did I mention that she was exceptionally strong?

"He lays it on too thick. Any man who does that probably has ulterior motives."

I wondered if Carole's ex had been lacking in the sweet endearments side of things. Of course, Carole didn't exactly encourage them.

"Well, you'll have to bring me more in the way of evidence than just your suspicions before I'll try to take away what might be Mrs. Hazlet's last chance at happiness."

Carole gave a contemptuous "humph" and returned to the dining room.

Aside from taking Dynamite up and down the block in front of the inn for his morning walk, I spent the rest of my time mentally rehearsing what I was going to say to Brianna when she showed up demanding a report. I hate to disappoint people, but either way I went on this one I'd be disappointing someone. Either Brianna or Rachel would feel that I had done wrong when she learned the truth. And, in my experience, when you were doing something sneaky, people almost invariably come to learn the truth.

Five minutes before noon, just as my hands were beginning to sweat in anticipation of having to lie, the Wentworths, a couple that was supposed to show up late in the afternoon, arrived and wanted to know if they could get into their suite early. Just as they approached the counter, Brianna entered the lobby. Seeing I was busy, she drifted over to a rack of tourist brochures just inside the front door.

I used my cell phone to call up to the third floor and ask Gabriella if the Wentworth suite had been cleaned.

"*Todo listo,*" she replied, which I took to mean that it was ready for occupancy.

While the Wentworths were filling out their registration form, I picked my cell phone up from the counter and quickly took a picture of Brianna as she stood by the rack. It was only a three-quarters view of her face but in focus. I wasn't sure why I did it, but somehow I thought that I might need it for evidence in the future.

When the Wentworths were done with the paperwork, I sent them on their way, lugging their suitcases up to the third floor. I told them that Gabriella would be up there to answer any questions they might have. I didn't see the need to share with them that only if they were lucky would the answers be in English. Otherwise, they would be couched in indecipherable Spanish.

Once the lobby was empty, Brianna slowly made her way up to the desk.

"Good morning, Max," she said with a businesslike smile. "Have you had any success?"

"Well, I've called all the establishments that were on my list. A few of them refused to tell me if anyone by the name of Rachel McCall was either a resident or employed there, but the majority answered and said that she was not."

"I wonder if she could have gotten a false ID that she's using to register."

"Not every B&B and hotel checks IDs carefully. She could possibly have gotten away with signing in under a false name." I thought of Mrs. Hardy who ran the Sea View B&B. Her vision was such that she'd have accepted a picture of your cat as ID. "The other possibility is that Rachel rented a condo though a realtor. Realtors aren't on my list."

"How many do you think there are in town?" Brianna asked.

"Around ten."

"Could you use that," she asked, pointing at my computer, "to generate a list of realtors? I'll check them out myself."

A minute later, I'd printed out the list the search engine had generated.

"I'll interview these people personally." She pushed a small pile of bills across the desk. "This is two hundred for your services. If I need your help again, I'll let you know."

"Thank you," I replied, not quite meeting her eyes out of guilt. "I hope you find your sister."

"Oh, I'm sure I will . . . eventually."

I still felt guilty about accepting money for a job I hadn't done. As I stuffed the bills in my pants pocket, I eased my conscience by telling myself that I'd indirectly earned the money by helping Rachel deal with her problem.

I tried to put the matter out of my head by opening up the emails—most of which were business related or spam—until my eyes fell on one that wasn't either one.

Max,

What's this I hear about Mrs. Hazlet leaving? I will be at the inn two days from now.

Uncle Edward

I immediately knew how Uncle Edward had learned this information, and the source was coming around the counter at just this moment.

"So, I see you couldn't resist going behind my back and contacting my uncle," I said to Carole. "Even though I told you not to."

"I don't take orders from you," she said defiantly. "I thought Edward had a right to know. I was protecting him."

"No, you were trying to wangle my job."

"Only because I deserve it and can do it a lot better than you."

I wanted to tell her to go to hell but didn't quite have the nerve. I wished I knew how to say it in Spanish, that I could probably manage to do because it would be less confrontational. I'd have to ask Gabriella the next time I saw her.

"Now why don't you run away back to your apartment and let me take care of things out front," Carole said.

I thought about refusing to obey, but then I'd be left standing behind the desk next to her like a sulky child. I spun around and walked away toward my apartment. Dynamite got off his cushion by the fireplace and quickly joined me as I marched across the lobby. Gabriella was coming down the stairs just as I reached them.

"What's the Spanish for 'Go to hell?'" I asked.

She gave me her patented unflappable look. "¡Vete al infierno!"

"Good," I said, repeating it several times to myself. "I think I'll try to memorize that."

I figured that was a phrase that could come in handy in the hospitality industry.

Chapter Eight

Four o'clock found Dynamite and myself walking up and down past the Gray Gull Inn. Up and down we went, until even Dynamite seemed to have exhausted all the smells in that small bit of real estate. When four-fifteen arrived and Rachel still hadn't put in an appearance, I decided that direct action was necessary. Tying Dynamite's leash to a column on the porch, I walked into the lobby and up to the desk. A middle-aged woman gave me a shrewd look.

"Can I help you?" she asked.

"I hope so," I said, giving her my best puzzled little boy smile that some older women found endearing.

I'd used it a lot when I played in *No Bells for Bing*o where I was a young, somewhat simpleminded, English aristocrat who finally learns the true meaning of Christmas. One critic said that I was made for the role.

"My sister, Rachel McCall, works here, and I was wondering if I could see her."

The woman gave me a kindly smile. "I'm sorry, but Rachel doesn't work here anymore. In fact, she quit just this morning without warning. It came as something of a surprise."

"Oh. This was the only address that I had for her. Would you be able to tell me where she lives?"

"I'm sorry, but we can't give out that kind of confidential information about our former employees."

"Perhaps her phone number?"

She shook her head firmly. "But if you give me your name, I will get in touch with her and give her a message. She can get back to you then."

I could see that this woman was no pushover. "Okay. Just tell her that Max needs to speak with her as soon as possible." I gave the woman my cell phone number. I thanked her rather effusively to encourage her to make the call and left.

"What do you think of that Dynamite?" I asked as we walked away from the inn.

He looked up at me but didn't express an opinion.

I returned to the Fireside Inn and made myself supper in my apartment. I always kept the door between my apartment and the lobby opened a crack in case a guest needed me. In fact, it was hardly necessary to keep the door open because the Chinese gong that Uncle Edward had mounted at the end of the reservations desk for guests to strike if they needed help when no one was at the desk could easily be heard in Beijing.

After eating, I went over my script for *The Butler Did It!* We were opening in four days, and the first dress rehearsal was tomorrow night. My nineteen thirties-style tux was in my closet, and I was set to go as far as knowing my lines. But I still felt that there were some areas where I could deliver them with more nuance. Acting is all in the details. I spent a couple of hours saying them out loud to myself until my eyes began to close, indicating that it was time to go to bed.

I took Dynamite out for a final walk around the garden. I fluffed up the pillow he had grown so attached to and made sure his water bowl was full. After turning in a circle he settled comfortably into his corner of my bedroom. I went through the lobby and locked the front door. Guests could still get in with their keys, but passing strangers would be kept out. Then I returned to my apartment, carefully locking the door between it and the lobby. I'd occasionally had guests come wandering into my apartment for amorous reasons, both men and women, so I had become very careful about the matter. After I was done in my en suite bathroom, I got into bed and said goodnight to Dynamite, who gave a muffled woof in reply. For a few moments I let my lines flow thorough my head, hoping that my subconscious would thoroughly cement everything I had practiced into my mind. Then I was asleep.

I was dreaming that something hard was pressing into my forehead. I tried to turn my head away, but the irritation persisted.

"Lie still, and I might not kill you," a woman's voice said.

The light on my bedside table went on, and I saw Brianna standing over me. A gun with an exceptionally long barrel was pressed against my forehead. I crossed my eyes and saw that a silencer was attached to the barrel. I guess technically it was a suppressor because it doesn't actually silence sound, I told myself. Funny the things your mind dredges up from television when you're paralyzed with fear.

"What are you doing here?" I asked through a mouth filled with cotton.

"Didn't you think I would know that you were lying to me? And sending me on that wild goose chase to all those realtors, that . . . was . . . not . . . nice." She gave me a staccato rap on the forehead in time with each word. I also noticed that a faint Hispanic accent had crept into her voice. I wondered if Gabriella's ambience had somehow contaminated the entire inn. "I should kill you for that alone."

"Um. I'd rather you didn't," I said.

"Maybe I won't if you tell me all that you have discovered about Rachel McCall."

"She was working as a waitress at the Gray Gull Inn. I spoke with her, and she said that she didn't have a sister," I said, proving that I'd never be able to conceal information under torture.

Brianna (or whatever her real name was) chuckled. "Yes. Our relationship is a bit more strained than that. Where is Rachel now?"

"I don't know."

She again shoved the suppressor hard into my forehead. I could only hope that stage makeup would be able to conceal the bruise at tomorrow's rehearsal.

"Do you prefer to die?"

"No. I really don't know where she is. I returned to the Gray Gull this afternoon, but she had quit her job. They wouldn't tell me where she lived or give me a phone number."

"Well, I guess this is it, then," she said, drawing a bead on my face.

"Really, that's all I know."

She gave me a sorrowful smile. "I believe you," she said, her finger beginning to tighten on the trigger.

They say your whole life flashes before you when you're about to die. But all I could see was the end of the barrel. I wondered if I would see the bullet coming at me in slow motion like in the movies. Maybe that way I could dodge it. I felt something bounce on the bed, and suddenly the gun disappeared from my field of vision. A creature of fur and teeth had jumped over me and locked onto Brianna's right wrist. She yelped as Dynamite growled and shook his head as if killing some vermin, which in this case was sort of on point. Brianna reached over with her left and grabbed a handful of fur and tore Dynamite off her. He gave a cry of pain.

I sprang into action. I reached forward and began to twist the gun from her grip. We struggled for a few seconds. There was a loud pfft! and my bedside lamp exploded. But now the gun was in my hand. I heard a scrambling sound, and by the time I had rolled to the other side of the bed and turned on that lamp, my room was empty. Holding the gun in front of me like some kind of talisman, I searched my small apartment. Brianna was gone. I spotted the small hole over the lock in the window of my back door where she had gained entrance. I promised myself I'd have that window repaired and a less accessible deadbolt added by the end of the day tomorrow as I jammed a chair tightly under the doorknob.

I returned to my room and looked for Dynamite. He was back on his pillow. I checked him over. Aside from looking a bit insulted, he seemed fine. I gave him a good petting, along with numerous accolades, all variations on "good dog." Then he had a dog treat, while I indulged in a bowl of ice cream.

I thought that after the night we'd had, we both deserved a midnight snack.

Chapter Nine

"Take it again from the top," Sergeant Azure Blue said, removing the cell phone from her ear as she walked back into the lobby. She'd stepped out in front of the inn to make a call after I'd given her the first account of my story. Now she was sounding very much like Mrs. Federico, who frequently demanded that I "take it again from the top" when she wasn't suggesting that I "grow a pair."

I carefully went through the events one more time from when I had agreed to work for Brianna until my near-death experience of last night.

"Let me get this straight, you decided to pretend to be a detective in order to help this hit woman kill someone named Rachel McCall, who has now disappeared."

"Rachel may still be around, but I don't know where. Otherwise, your summary is substantially correct."

"This doesn't put you in a very good light, Max."

"I was duped."

"How often have you used that excuse in your life?"

A low blow, but I had to admit to myself that I'd used it more often than I cared to admit. I tended to expect the best of people and often didn't see through to their ulterior motives. Sergeant Blue reached in the case she had brought with her and took out a large plastic bag.

"Let's see the gun."

I led her across the lobby and into my apartment. Dynamite trailed along behind as if he had to act as my chaperone. The gun was on the table where I had left it the night before.

The sergeant gave it a long look.

"Pretty impressive. I've never seen one in real life before, but that certainly looks like a suppressor. Your friend must be a professional."

"She's no friend of mine."

"Not now, but you did agree to help her."

I couldn't argue with that.

Sergeant Blue took a piece of cloth from her case and carefully placed the gun in the large plastic bag.

"We'll have the county lab check the prints on it. To eliminate yours, I'll have to fingerprint you."

We moved over to the dresser. She took out an inkpad and a piece of paper divided up into sections for each finger. She carefully inked my fingers and pressed each one down firmly on the appropriate spot.

"Big departments can do this electronically where you just press down on a keypad. But we're still old school," she said, as I cleaned my fingers off with a tissue. "Still, we might get lucky and find out who this Brianna is who tried to kill you."

"I have a picture of her," I said.

She gave me a long look. "I'm glad you finally mentioned it. How did you manage that?"

I explained how I got the photo of her standing by the rack of brochures in the lobby. I showed her the picture on my phone.

"Not a great shot, but a lot better than nothing." She asked me to send it to her phone and I did.

We walked back out to the lobby.

"Part of her story must have been true," I said. "She probably did hire Jenkins to find Rachel. When he died, she decided to take the job on herself with my assistance. Don't you think you'd better notify the Gray Gull Inn that a killer might be paying them a visit looking for Rachel's address?"

"Already called. The woman who answered said no one had been around looking for Rachel, except for her brother yesterday. I take it that was you?"

I nodded sheepishly.

"A uniformed officer should be there by now to keep an eye on things until I get there. I'll check on Rachel's address and phone number. The sooner we find her, the sooner we can protect her."

"She may have ditched her phone and moved by now," I said. "She seemed pretty skittish the other night."

"She may be long gone from Lighthouse Point, but if she's still in town. I think we'll find her."

I nodded.

Azure Blue gave me a small smile. "How's the play going?"

"We begin dress rehearsals tonight. Opening night is on Saturday. Are you still planning to come?"

"I wouldn't miss it. Who wouldn't want to watch a mystery where the butler actually did it?"

I nodded enthusiastically. "It's very avant-garde."

"I'm sure," she said dryly, taking her bag and heading out the door.

"Who was that?"

I jumped. Carole was standing next to me. She really was very skillful at sneaking up on people.

"A police detective," I answered, hoping she wouldn't ask more, but knowing that she would. She'd unerringly sense this as an opportunity to make me look bad.

"Why was she here?" Carole asked predictably.

"Someone tried to break in through the back door to my apartment last night. Whoever it was cut a hole in the glass, but I heard the noise and the culprit ran away. I'm having the glass replaced and a new double-key deadbolt installed."

She gave me a suspicious look as if I weren't telling her the whole story, which, of course, I wasn't.

"I'm surprised they sent a detective for that."

I shrugged. "I knew Sergeant Blue from before when she was looking into Mr. Jenkins's death. I think she came along as a favor to me."

Carole gave me a look suggesting that the only favor she'd do for me is to give directions to the unemployment line. Then she headed back to the dining room.

Since the lobby was quiet after the breakfast rush, I took Dynamite for a walk up the street. He stopped to admire every tree, while I paused to appreciate the Victorian houses that lined both sides of the street. Although almost 150 years old and often a maintenance nightmare, to me these houses represented a previous way of life that had a grace and charm missing today. I often thought that I would have done better in that more gentle and polite era. The rough and tumble of today often left me bruised and battered. I looked southeast where I could see the blue of the Atlantic on the horizon. The idea that it had always been there and always would somehow comforted me.

My cell phone rang. I fished it out of my pocket, hoping that it wasn't someone wanting to book a room, since I was away from the desk and had no access to the computer.

"Max, is that you?" a woman asked.

"Yes," I whispered, although there was no one standing nearby. I knew Rachel's voice when I heard it.

"I need your help, Max. I don't know what to do."

"Whatever you do, don't go back to the Gray Gull Inn," I told her. Then I gave her a bare bones account of my confrontation with Brianna.

"She tried to kill you?" Rachel asked.

"And almost succeeded. I think it would be wise if you moved from where you are presently living. Brianna is trying to find your address, and she seems very persistent."

"I've already moved and purchased a prepaid phone. Are the police looking for me now too?"

"Yes, but I think you have less to fear from them."

"But I'm not sure I'd be safe even with them if Brianna and the man she works for find out where I am."

"Where are you?"

"I can't tell you, Max."

"I wouldn't betray you."

"Even if your life depended on it."

I paused. "Good point. But I think I deserve an explanation of what this is all about."

There was a long pause. "Meet me in the parking lot behind the Busted Beacon tonight at ten, and I'll tell you everything. Make sure you aren't followed."

I agreed. My dress rehearsal would easily be over by nine-thirty because it wasn't a complete run through. We were only working on the last act.

After Rachel ended the call, I stood on the street looking at nothing for a long while, wondering whether I really wanted to hear her story. I'll admit that I was curious, but that just reminded me of the old saying about curiosity and dead cats. Dynamite looked at me as if to say that he had no strong opinions about either one.

Chapter Ten

I returned to the inn, still thinking about my meeting with Rachel tonight. I tried to come up with a way in which I could get her to tell me where she was staying, but nothing came to me. Since there wasn't anything much going on in the lobby, I decided to go into the kitchen and see how Mrs. Hazlet was doing. She always seemed to appreciate a daily visit from me and would often have some suggestions for new breakfast items.

When I came into the kitchen, Randolph Fuller was sitting at the counter next to Mrs. Hazlet, both had coffee cups in front of them. They looked up when I entered and slid slightly further apart.

"Good morning, Mrs. H," I said. "How are you this morning, Mr. Fuller?"

"Call me Randy," he said.

I suspected he was.

"Don't let me disturb you," I said, not quite able to make it sound sincere.

"That's okay, my boy, I was just telling Emily about the Louvre in Paris and how it's well worth the visit if only to see the Mona Lisa."

"I'm certain that it is. Do you travel a lot in your line of work?" I asked.

"Not internationally. That I do for fun," he said, giving Mrs. H a broad wink. "I'm a wealth manager in the New York area, so I do a lot of traveling in the vicinity of the city."

"You're fortunate to have the time and money to travel to Europe."

"Well, I can pretty much set my own schedule, so if I work really hard for a few months, I can usually manage to take a couple of weeks off. As far as money goes, it's all relative. I'm not nearly as wealthy as my clients, many of whom are multimillionaires, but I do pretty well. I'll be retiring in a few years and have more time for that sort of thing. The only thing that's kept me working this long is that I'm a widower, and I've been looking for someone to share my life with before I retire."

He smiled at Mrs. H, who blushed but reached over and patted is hand.

I asked Mrs. H if she had any business matters to discuss, which of course she didn't. As I left the kitchen, I thought to myself that one thing Carole and I agreed on was that Uncle Edward's relationship with Mrs. H was in dire jeopardy.

Later in the morning, I was standing at the desk going through our monthly bookings, which were up 50 percent over last year's at the same time. I attributed this to my new advertising program. I only hoped the increase in income would cover the cost of the ads and leave a sizable profit.

Sergeant Blue came in the door and marched up to the desk. She was wearing an oxford shirt, chinos, and a blazer, which made her look very preppy, although I suspected she wore the blazer to conceal the gun on her hip.

"Got some information for you, Max," she announced without preliminaries. "I sent the picture of the woman calling herself Brianna off to the FBI. Her picture matched one they have on file for *La Loba*."

"Excuse me," I said, thinking I had suddenly drifted into a conversation with Gabriella.

"Yeah, it's Spanish for the She Wolf. Apparently, that's her professional name. Guess you would call it a stage name. No one knows anything much about her. Apparently, she's a hired assassin and is thought to be responsible for a number of murders. The FBI thinks she advertises over the dark web. Guess that shows the benefits of advertising."

I wondered if there was a section on the dark web for B&Bs.

"I've sent out your picture of her to the entire force here in town so they can keep their eyes open for her. No one is authorized to approach her without a lot of backup. She's one dangerous character." The sergeant smiled. "Of course, on that one I suppose I'm preaching to the choir."

"She is scary," I said, feeling a small shiver travel down my spine. "You don't think she'll come back here, do you?"

"Not unless you're hiding Rachel McCall in one of your upstairs rooms," Blue said with a short laugh.

"Have you had any luck finding Rachel?" I asked.

The sergeant shook her head. "She's moved out of her room that she gave at the Gray Gull, and we haven't had any luck tracing her cell phone. She's probably trashed that as well. I guess she's afraid of anyone finding her. I don't blame her. We just got a report from the police in Brooklyn where she was living after I ran her name through the system. Her roommate, Gina Martin, was murdered. It happened a few days ago, but they just found her body yesterday. The police said there were signs of torture. I guess that's how *La Loba* found out that Rachel had come here." Blue gave me a suspicious glance. "You don't happen to know where Rachel is staying now?"

I shook my head. "No idea," I said, happy that I could truthful answer that narrowly asked question.

She nodded and smiled. "Do you have a rehearsal tonight?"

"The first dress rehearsal."

"Well, break a leg, as we say in the business."

I nodded and gave her a weak smile.

No sooner had Sergeant Blue gone out the door, leaving me somewhat rattled, than my nemesis, Carole, slipped behind the desk and crept up behind me as she likes to do.

"Edward should be here by tomorrow," she said in a loud voice that made me jump.

"If he shows up at all," I replied, once I had caught my breath.

"Oh, he'll be here all right," she assured me. "He's not about to lose Mrs. H to some smooth talker from the big city. And he won't be happy that you didn't tell him about it."

"We'll see," I replied, falling back on my usual snappy retort.

"That we will," she said gaily, as if she already saw herself standing in my place.

*****

After lunch, I spent the rest of the afternoon running through my lines, hoping to give a polished performance of the last act this evening. Intermittently, I wondered what I would do if Carole was right, and I had to look for another job. HVAC with Dad and my brothers was certainly out. Every brain cell I had would be completely fried within a month. I had also come to accept the fact that I had given acting a fair shot, and it would never provide me with enough income to live. I could send my resume out to other B&Bs in Lighthouse Point, but I doubted my chances. Gossip spreads quickly in a small resort community, and when word got out that my own uncle had fired me, that would hardly be a good reference.

Toward the end of the afternoon, I took Dynamite out for a walk. As we strolled along the rather quiet back streets of Lighthouse Point, I told Dynamite about my employment issues. He occasionally glanced up, encouraging me to give him all the details. When I was done, he gently brushed against my leg as if to indicate that I was stressing about something that hadn't happened yet and that I should relax. I decided he was probably right. There was no reason for me to assume that Carole's dire prediction about my future employment status would ever be true. After all, the inn was doing well financially, and I had been very conscientious in my stewardship. There was no cause for panic, none at all.

As we walked into the lobby of the inn, Mr. Fuller walked past us, heading out. I heard a low growl from Dynamite. I was surprised because he almost never behaved that way. Of course, Mrs. H had gotten in the habit of giving him the occasional tasty treat from the kitchen. Maybe he in some way sensed that Fuller was a threat to take away his source of future culinary delights by getting Mrs. H to run away with him. You can never be certain how much dogs know about their environment.

After a light supper—I always get slightly nauseous on the first night of dress rehearsals—I changed into my tux and headed over to the church. Everyone was there earlier than usual and milling around looking slightly self-conscious in the period dress.

Mrs. Federico came over and gave me an admiring glance. "You clean up very well, Max. It's just too bad . . ." She shook her head and walked away. I knew she was thinking how unfortunate it was that I didn't have the manly personality to fit my looks.

The run-through of the final act went rather smoothly for me. I knew my lines perfectly and had nicely styled my delivery to be appropriate to a gentleman detective from the thirties. I even spotted Chelsea, out of the corner of my eye, giving me an admiring glance.

The only problem arose at the very end of the act. As you may recall, I had to poke Rick in the chest and accuse him of being the murderer. Right after that, he was supposed to pull out a gun from behind his back. I then had to wrestle it from him and slap a pair of cuffs on his wrists. After all that action, I was directed to turn, walk downstage to the audience, and say in a strong voice, "As you see, this time the butler really did do it."

All went swimmingly. I gave Rick a firm, but not painful, finger to the chest and accused him of being a murderer. He then pulled out the prop gun from behind his back, but instead of cooperating with me as I attempted to wrestle it away, as we had practiced, he resisted. Not wanting to hurt him, we went dancing across the stage as I tried to gently pull the gun from his hand.

"Cut," Mrs. Federico yelled. She walked up to the stage and shook her head in disgust. "This is not supposed to be a wrestling match gentlemen. Work out how you are going to do it and coordinate your actions. Rick, behave yourself, and Max . . ." She just shook her head, which again I knew meant that I should "grow a pair."

I hurried away at the end of rehearsals, partly to see Rachel and partly not wanting to see Rick's smirking face or Chelsea's sympathetic glance. Although I haven't got much of a temper, Rick was certainly trying what little I had.

Chapter Eleven

I spent some time cooling my heels in the parking lot behind the Busted Beacon. I was just about to believe that Rachel had changed her mind about showing up when I heard a voice from behind a large bush on the edge of the parking lot.

"Is that you, Max?" the bush asked.

I turned to face it. "Of course it is. Is that you, Rachel?"

"Of course, who do you think it is, God?" Rachel came out from behind cover and walked toward me, her head swiveling around to take in the entire parking lot.

"Are you alone?"

"I certainly hope so."

By the glow of the lights, I saw her frown. She was probably hoping for greater certainty.

"Why are you dressed like that?" she said, looking up and down at my tux. "You look like James Bond."

"I'm Moran, Max Moran," I said in a poor imitation of every actor who's ever played the spy.

She didn't smile.

"I had a dress rehearsal tonight for a play I'm in," I replied, taking a moment to study her. She was looking rather bedraggled, and her hair was mussed. "You're not looking too good."

"I had to leave my apartment. I slept on the beach last night to save money. I'll be broke in a few days now that I had to give up my job. I tried to call my roommate to wire me some money, but I didn't get an answer. So naturally, I'm not looking my best."

"Would that be Gina Martin?"

"How did you know?"

"The police sergeant who came to see me today told me that the police in Brooklyn found Gina's body in your apartment. She'd been murdered."

I didn't see any reason to mention the torture, but even without that, Rachel began to pitch forward, and I just managed to catch her in my arms. I gave her a long hug. I could feel her body shaking as she sobbed. After a long moment, she stepped away from me.

"Gina was a good friend," she said between sniffs. "They must have threatened her to find out where I had gone. I shouldn't have told her."

"It wouldn't have mattered. *La Loba* would have killed her anyway. She knew about the murder."

"Who?"

"The woman calling herself Brianna is a hired assassin called *La Loba*, The She Wolf."

"God! What am I going to do?"

"Why don't we walk back under the trees where we won't be seen, and you tell me who is after you and why. Maybe then we can come up with a plan to protect you."

We drifted into the shadows of the tree line and checked to be sure we weren't visible from the street. Rachel picked her backpack off the ground and slung it over her shoulder.

"So who is after you?" I repeated.

"A man named Sidney Chase. He's the owner of the finance company where I worked. One night about three weeks ago, I was working late and no one knew I was there. I heard some shouting down the hall. I went to check. It was coming from Mr. Chase's office, and when I opened the door, he was standing there holding a sports trophy and on the floor at his feet was Stan Spiegel, his partner. I just knew right away that he had murdered him, and from the look on his face, I could tell he wanted to do the same to me. So I turned and ran. I raced down the fire stairs. I could hear him pounding along behind me, but I'm a fast runner. I got away and went back to my apartment. I threw some stuff in my backpack and told Gina what happened and that I was off to the southernmost point on the Jersey shore. I asked her to tell anyone who came looking for me that she had never seen me that night, then I got the last bus out of the city. When I didn't hear anything for three weeks, I thought I was safe. That was until you showed up with the story about my sister Brianna."

"Chase must have decided to hire a professional to hunt you down. I wonder how he would have known how to go about doing that so quickly."

"Well, although they called the business a finance company, some pretty unsavory characters used to hang out around the place. It made me so uncomfortable that I was planning to quit."

"Probably they were more into loan sharking than home mortgage loans. Chase had contacts that could put him on to a hired assassin."

Rachel shook her head sadly. "I should have left the job sooner, but they paid really well."

"We've all regretted at some time in our lives that we took a job just for the money."

"But what am I going to do now? I have nowhere to live. I can't keep sleeping on the beach and wandering the streets. This killer will eventually find me."

"Maybe I can help," I said slowly. "I might be able to offer you a place to stay."

Rachel touched me on the shoulder. "That's very kind of you but staying at your inn wouldn't work very well. People would notice me, and I have a feeling that this Spanish killer will be checking up on you every once in a while."

That was a thought that made me shiver. I was tempted to wash my hands of the whole thing and tell Rachel to turn herself in to the police for protection. I could hardly believe what I said next.

"That's not a problem. I have a small apartment over the garage behind the inn. No one will ever see you there."

I paused and took a deep breath. All of Mrs. Federico's admonitions about "growing a pair" were apparently starting to seep into my real life for good or ill.

"Are you sure?" Rachel asked.

I resisted saying that I'd only been kidding. "You can hide there for a few days. I can probably scrape together enough money to send you somewhere far out of town. If this guy Chase doesn't find you in another week, he'll probably figure that he's safe and stop the search."

"Well, I guess it's the best chance that I've got."

We walked back to the inn, pausing every once in a while to look and listen, making sure we weren't being followed. The gaslights that the tourism committee used to illuminate the streets in the historic section of town made it difficult to see much, but they also made it difficult to be seen. We walked past the inn and around the corner. The two-car garage that went with the inn faced on the side street. We slipped around the back of the garage and up the outside wooden staircase to the apartment above.

I unlocked the door and we went inside.

"We'd better not turn on the lights. The neighbors around here are nosey. If they see lights, they might call the police. I had a small flashlight on my keychain and by its narrow beam, I showed Rachel around the apartment.

"I know it's not much," I admitted.

"It's better than sleeping on the beach."

We checked out the cabinets. The refrigerator had been turned off, so I put it back on.

"You'll need food. I'll bring something over from my apartment early in the morning for breakfast. I'll buy more groceries for you later in the day."

"Who used to live here?" she asked.

"Jim. He was an older man who had been the handyman and gardener here from back before my Uncle Edward bought the place."

"What happened to him?"

"He died."

"In this apartment."

"Right in the bed, actually. He had a stroke." I paused. "I hope that doesn't spook you."

"I guess not. As long as I don't end up the same way."

I patted her arm. "We're doing our best to avoid that." I checked my watch. It was getting close to the time for Lexi to go off duty. "I'll see you tomorrow. There are sheets in that closet to make the bed. And here's a flashlight," I said, taking one out of a kitchen drawer.

"Thanks very much for everything," Rachel said, giving me a brief hug.

"It's the least I could do since I led the killer right to you. I'll see you in the morning."

I walked back around the building and in through the front door of the inn. Lexi stood up behind the counter when she heard the door open.

"How did the rehearsal go?" she asked.

"Pretty well. I think we'll be ready by Saturday."

Lexi sighed. "I can't imagine doing anything like that."

"Like what?"

"Standing in front of a room full of people and talking. I know I'd just sweat all over."

"Are you sure that a career as an anchorperson is right for you?" I asked gently.

"Oh, that's different. You just look into the camera, and you don't actually see the people. There are only a handful of folks in the studio anyway."

"I suppose you're right," I said, trying to keep the doubt out of my voice.

"Well, I'd better be going now," she said, putting a couple of books in her backpack. "The next rehearsal is the day after tomorrow?"

"Right. Can you cover the desk then?"

"No problem."

As she walked across the lobby to leave, I wondered if she was deluding herself in her career choice. Self-delusion is such a common thing. I'd been guilty of it myself a number of times in my life.

I wondered if I was repeating that pattern by thinking that I could keep Rachel safe from a professional killer. I decided that I had to make arrangements to get her out of town very soon or else we both might end up like poor old Jim.

Chapter Twelve

I got up earlier than usual the next morning. I packed a jar of milk, a box of cold cereal, and a couple of slices of bread in a plastic bag. There wasn't much in my apartment in the way of breakfast makings because I usually had Mrs. H cook me something early in the morning before the normal breakfast serving time began. I had a particular weakness for her pancakes. She'd taken to warning me that I wouldn't be able to eat the way I did once I reached thirty and my metabolism slowed. She warned that I might even have to embark on an exercise program. I thought that suggestion was particularly cruel.

Taking Dynamite with me as an excuse for being out so early, I slipped over behind the garage and up the back stairs. I tapped lightly on the door. About a minute passed, and the door opened a crack.

"I brought you something for breakfast," I said.

She opened the door wider and took the bag. She was wearing a long sweatshirt.

"Did you sleep well?" I asked.

"As well as can be expected considering. Not quite as well as Jim did." She smiled to show she was joking.

"Thank goodness. I'll be back later in the morning with more food. I'll try to come up with a plan to get you out of town."

She nodded. She shut the door and I hurried down the stairs, hoping that all the nosey neighbors were sleeping in. Spending a few more minutes letting Dynamite do the necessaries in the garden, I came back in through my apartment and gave him breakfast. After that, Dynamite returned to his usual spot near the fireplace, while I went into the kitchen to have breakfast for myself.

"What will you be having this morning, Max?" Mrs. H asked as I entered the kitchen.

I'd seen a bit of the sparkle disappear from her eyes when she saw that I was the one coming into the kitchen instead of Fuller.

"I guess I'll have a couple of pancakes."

She shook her head. "Maybe you should just have a single slice of toast and an egg. You've got to watch that waistline of yours, you know."

I patted my flat stomach. "I don't see much to worry about there."

"Not right now, maybe. But in a few more years, when your metabolism slows down, you'll start to see the results of all this easy living." She smiled slightly as she always did at her ritualistic joke.

"Well, when I start seeing those results, I guess I'll have to cut down to one-and-a-half pancakes. You know how I love your pancakes," I said, getting into the swing of things.

She chuckled and put the pancake mixture on the griddle. She studied the grill carefully, as if she had never seen it before.

"I'm really sorry that Carole told Edward about my friendship with Randy. If Edward does come up from Florida, it will look like I'm purposely pitting the two of them against each other like some high school girl. If Edward couldn't be bothered to leave his golf behind in over a year to come up and see me, I really don't want him here now just because he's jealous."

She flipped two pancakes onto a plate for me and put genuine maple syrup and some butter on the table next to them. I settled down at the kitchen table and began to tuck in.

"I can appreciate what you're saying," I said, chewing my first mouthful. "How do you really feel about Randy Fuller?"

She paused with the spatula in her hand and stared across the kitchen. "I'm not completely sure. It's very flattering, of course, to be taken out to nice restaurants and given flowers by an attractive man. But I don't feel that I know him very well."

"I thought he'd told you a lot about himself."

"He does talk quite a bit, but somehow I don't really feel that I know him." She shook her head. "How much do you ever know someone? I'd worked with Edward for ten years, from when he first bought this inn. I thought there were no surprises left. Then he took off for Florida to play golf all the time."

"Was it really that much of a surprise? From what I heard from Mom, he'd drifted off a few times in the ten years that he's owned the inn."

"Sure. But those times he was always involved in some sort of business opportunity. Starting new businesses is his real strength. But golf? I mean, he'd always enjoyed golf, but who thought he'd want to compete in some amateur senior's tour."

"New worlds to conquer," I guess.

Mrs. H just shook her head.

"Will you take him back if he returns and asks?"

She gave me a shrewd glance. "I'll have to weigh my options. Things certainly aren't going to go back to the way they were."

As I finished my pancakes, I thought to myself that Uncle Edward was going to find that things at the Fireside Inn were not the way he had left them.

I stayed behind the desk until most of the guests had gone in to breakfast. Then I planned to take the car and run over to the local supermarket to get some supplies for Rachel. Gabriella was in by then, and since she couldn't start cleaning the rooms for another hour or so, I asked if she would answer the phone if anyone called while I was out. She glanced up from checking her messages on her phone.

"*No es mi trabajo,*" she replied.

"Which means?" I asked.

"Not my job."

"Would you like to continue having a job?"

She frowned. "You have no sense of humor."

"Right. Don't wander off and answer the phone politely if someone calls." I paused for a moment. "And answer in English."

"What if they speak Spanish?"

"Particularly then." Her Spanish would insult an entire culture.

She gave me a pouty look and flounced over behind the desk.

I went through my apartment, taking Dynamite with me. I figured he could come with me on the short trip to the supermarket. It would give him a chance to see more of his hometown. I walked through the garden to the garage and pulled up the door. Uncle Edward's blue BMW sat in the bay. It was his second car. He had taken his Mustang to Florida with him. One of my responsibilities was to take Beamer out for a drive every so often. I'm sure most men would have considered driving a BMW around town to be a treat rather than a responsibility, but having spent much of my adult life living in New York City without a car, and living now in a small resort town where almost everything was within walking distance, I'd never developed much of an enthusiasm for driving.

I backed the car carefully out of the garage. Denting the BMW would be more of a threat to my job than Carole. With the window partly down, Dynamite seemed to enjoy all the sights and smells of living in a shore community. I quickly traveled the two miles to the market, and leaving the window down a crack for Dynamite, I went into the store to make my purchases.

Not being sure how long Rachel would be staying, I got the basics: milk, coffee, bread, bologna, pickles, processed cheese, and cookies. Not the foundation for the healthiest meal plan, but I figured Rachel had to worry about more immediate things than a bad diet killing her. After returning the car to the garage and putting Dynamite on the leash, I went up the back stairs of the garage, carefully looking around in case some nosey neighbor was out in their yard. I knocked softly on the door. It opened a crack, and two eyes peered out at me.

"I have some more food for you," I said.

Rachel opened the door a bit more, and I slipped inside.

"How are you doing?" I asked.

"Okay," she said dully.

I opened the bag and laid the food out on the small counter. She eyed my purchases warily. In my experience, young women worry excessively about what they eat, but then I can consume vast amounts without gaining a pound, so who am I to judge.

"I know it's not much, but I thought it would be enough to keep you going until we can get you out of town."

"When do you think that's going to happen? I feel like I'm sitting here just waiting for that crazy assassin to find me." She sighed. "I keep thinking about Gina, and how horrible it must have been for her."

I reached over and touched her arm. "That isn't going to happen to you."

"I wish I could believe that."

"I'll get some money ready today and check on the bus schedule out of town. You can go from here up to New York City, and from there you can travel by bus or train to anywhere. This guy Chase will never find you. I'll be in touch early tomorrow morning. I'll come and knock on the door."

She nodded, but I could see she still had her doubts. I may look like an action hero, but I don't always manage to convey quite the appropriate level of masculine confidence. It had been the curse of my acting career.

After a quick goodbye and a few more words of reassurance, Dynamite and I headed back down the stairs. We had just come out from behind the garage and headed back out to the walk that would take us to my apartment when someone called my name. It was Randy Fuller out for a morning's walk.

"You and your friend just out for a walk?" he asked.

"That's right," I replied, trying to detect if he suspected what I had actually been up to. Finding nothing, I said, "It's certainly a beautiful morning."

He nodded and walked closer to me. "I wanted to talk with you for a minute if you have the time. I heard that your uncle is coming back to town."

I gave a neutral nod.

"I gather that he and Emily were an item."

"They had a relationship for quite some time."

He frowned and glanced across the garden. "Do you think she still cares for him?"

"You'd have to ask her. I'm no expert on how women think."

Randy gave a snort. "What man is? Let me ask you this, why do you think your uncle is coming back from Florida right now? Is he going to try to win Emily back?"

I shrugged. "Uncle Edward never talks about his feelings. All he talks about are his adventures in high tech and golf. So I have no idea why he's returning right now. He could be coming to win Mrs. H back or he might just be here to check out how the inn is doing. It's hard to tell."

Fuller nodded. "Well, thanks for your time, Max." With that, he headed off again on his walk.

I walked back to my apartment thinking that love in one's older years wasn't that much different from high school infatuations. The same questions and concerns came up in each.

Chapter Thirteen

In the middle of the morning, I was standing at the reception desk looking over our advertising brochure and trying to figure out how to say the same things in a different and more appealing way when a great clattering of metal came in the front door. I looked up as Uncle Edward strode into the lobby like a conquering hero with his golf bag slung over one shoulder. He tossed his keys to me in a high arc. I just managed to catch them before they hit me in the face.

"Bring my luggage in, Max. I'm double-parked out front, and then put my car in the garage. Is my suite ready for me?"

"Sure is," I called out to his back, as he kept going up the stairs without awaiting an answer. I'd had Gabriella get his third-floor suite ready for him when I'd heard he was coming. You could never be too prepared for Uncle Edward.

He charged up the stairs—stopping only to give Dynamite a pat on the head, which the dog seemed to love—as if he were Sir Edmund Hilary, and he could see the peak of Everest lying straight ahead. Uncle Edward was rather portly and in his midfifties, but he had vigor to spare. I knew he'd hardly be breathing hard when he reached the third floor, even though he was carrying fifty pounds of clubs.

His full head of white hair and his slap-on-the-back humor seemed to endear him to dogs and men alike. Much of his success in business was probably due to his ability to convince other men, usually after a few drinks, that even his wildest schemes would result in unlimited financial success. From what my mother had told me about his earlier years, many women were also attracted by his testosterone-laced charm.

I waited behind the desk, pretending to work on something, but really anticipating my uncle's return. I didn't have to wait long. Within fifteen minutes he was bounding down the stairs and into the lobby carrying a gold club as if it were a cane.

"That Gabriella working on the third floor is a real pistol," he announced. "Although I have no idea what she's saying."

"Join the club," I said under my breath. "Do you want to go over the books?" I asked more loudly.

"Later, boy, later. Is Mrs. H. in the kitchen?"

I checked the grandfather clock across the room from the desk. "Breakfast ended half an hour ago, so she's probably in there cleaning up."

"Good. Good. I think I'll pay her a little visit and see how things are going."

Better you than me, I thought, as I watched him march into the dining room.

Fifteen minutes later he came charging back looking more florid than usual. Without recognizing my existence, he went out the front door and headed up the street. I had a feeling that his famous charm hadn't worked very well with Mrs. H.

I jumped when a hand touched my arm. I spun to my right, almost knocking over Carole who had snuck up next to me in her usual fashion. I took a deep breath to slow my racing heart.

"It was horrible," she said.

Like meeting you in a dark alley, I thought.

"What was?" I asked.

"The argument Mrs. H and Edward had in the kitchen."

"You just happened to be there," I said with a note of sarcasm.

She sniffed. "I happened to be standing by the door. After all, success in this day and age depends on having adequate information."

"I guess eavesdropping always works."

"Do you want to know what I heard or not?"

"Go ahead."

"Well, Edward started by saying that the word was around that Mrs. H was dating one of the guests. He said that he thought that violated the rules of proper professional behavior."

"What did she say to that?"

"She said she was a cook, not a doctor or a lawyer, and she could go out with whoever she wanted."

"I bet Uncle didn't like that."

"For a few seconds, all he did was sputter. Then he accused her of getting involved with some toy boy, and he said that there was no fool like an old fool. Mrs. H said that he was the old fool for running off in the dark of night to Florida, and she wasn't doing anything inappropriate."

"She has a point," I said. "What happened next?"

"Your uncle completely lost it. He said that if she couldn't treat the owner of the inn with proper respect, she shouldn't be working there. She said fine, and he should consider her to have given her two weeks' notice."

"Two weeks. How are we going to replace Mrs. H in that short a time?"

"It gets worse," Carole said grimly. "Edward said that two weeks' notice wouldn't be necessary, so Mrs. H said she would be gone by this Friday."

"Two days from now." I felt tightness in my chest and wondered if a vaguely fit man in his twenties could have a heart attack as a result of shock. "What are we going to do?"

Carole smirked. "Not 'we,' you're the manager. At least for right now."

She turned on her heel and pranced off like a show pony that knew it could win any competition, especially one against an old dray horse like me that had bulk but no imagination.

I racked my brain for the rest of the morning, between answering the phone and taking reservations, trying to come up with a solution to the cook problem. Since the summer season had already begun, there were very few skilled cooks who didn't already have a position. I could run an ad in the local paper, but the chances of getting someone in the next few days were extremely slim.

When Carole came in to take over the desk at noon, I asked her if she had any ideas. She gave me a coy smile.

"I used to be an assistant chef at the Grand Buffon when I was younger. So I've got some skills. But Edward wouldn't be willing to pay me enough to make it worth my while. Anyway, I'm going to be the next manager. Why would I take a lowly job as a cook?"

"What if you don't get to be manager? You've no guarantee that's going to happen."

"Then I'll go somewhere else where I'll be more appreciated. I've only been working here temporarily until something better opens up."

"There's nothing like loyalty."

"I'm loyal to myself."

I didn't have an answer to that.

Dynamite and I went back to my apartment and had some lunch. After lunch, I took him out for a short walk, then I told him that he'd have to stay alone in the apartment for a while because I had to go out. I went out the back door, so Carole wouldn't be able to question me about where I was going, and walked several blocks to the nearest branch of the bank where I kept my paltry savings. I didn't earn a lot, despite my exalted title as manager. The hospitality industry, like banking, tends to give titles as a substitute for payment, and Uncle Edward, like a lot of extremely wealthy people, tended to pinch the pennies until they sang falsetto. Also, I was still paying off student loans that had gotten me a degree from a good college that allowed me to live in genteel destitution.

I took as much money out of my savings as I could afford, maybe a little more. I figured it would be enough to get Rachel somewhere far away for a long enough time to outwait those who were after her. When I returned to the inn, I went in the front door, forgetting that I didn't want Carole to ask where I had been. She didn't because she had other things to occupy her mind.

"There's someone waiting for you," she announced, giving me a curious look and pointing to a chair near the fireplace.

Sergeant Azure Blue gave me a smile and a small wave.

"Before you get too comfy with your girlfriend, you should know that Edward wanted to see the books for the last year. I gave them to him, and he's in the dining room right now going over them in detail."

"Fine," I replied, trying to sound confident.

"He said that you should hang around because he'll want to see you once he's done."

"I'm not going anywhere."

I walked across the lobby to where Sergeant Blue was seated. "If you wouldn't mind, could we talk in my apartment where we'll have some privacy?"

"Sounds fine to me," she replied.

We went down the hall to my place and settled around the small kitchen table.

"Would you like something to drink?" I asked.

"Water would be fine. I've been wandering around town looking for *La Loba* most of the day. Finding an assassin is thirsty work."

I poured us two glasses of ice water and settled down across from her.

"Has she been spotted?" I asked.

"Not by anyone that I've talked to. The woman is like a ghost."

"But how can she hope to find Rachel if she's holed up somewhere?"

Azure shrugged. "Maybe she has help, a spotter or someone. But we're doing no better than she is. We can't find Rachel either."

I nodded, hoping I didn't look too guilty. "What about back in New York? Does anyone up there know where she's gone off to?"

"Not that we can find. Her roommate is dead, as you know. Her family lives in Maine, and they haven't heard from her. We tried to speak with her boss, but his secretary says that he's gone away on vacation and can't be reached."

I just bet he has, I thought.

"The reason I stopped by is that I wanted to ask about how the play is going," Sergeant Blue said. She gave me a rather shy smile. "I haven't forgotten that you promised me tickets."

"They're holding two at the box office for you. Just give them your name on opening night."

"Two?"

"I figured you might want to bring a date."

She smiled. "That's very thoughtful of you. But I'll probably be alone."

"No boyfriend right now, if you don't mind my asking?"

She shook her head. "I work with men all day. I prefer to be with girlfriends or by myself after work."

"But if the right man came along . . ."

"Maybe, but he'd have to be manly without being a jerk. That seems to be a challenge to find."

There was a knock on the door to my apartment.

"Sorry to bother you," Carole said when I opened the door. She flashed a smirk that told me she wasn't sorry at all. "But your Uncle Edward would like to see you now."

"I guess I'd better be leaving," Sergeant Blue said. She gave me a pat on the arm as we went out into the lobby. "Good luck on Saturday night."

"Thanks."

"If she's going out with you Saturday night, she's the one who will need the luck," Carole whispered.

I didn't deign to dignify that remark with a response.

"Where's Uncle Edward?" I asked.

"He's in the dining room, and he doesn't seem happy," she said, giving me a look of triumph.

Uncle Edward was on the far side of the dining room away from the door to the lobby. He was sitting at a round table with the inn's books piled up in front of him and his golf club by his side. When I entered the room, he glanced over and waved me toward the table.

"Have a seat, Max, I need to talk with you," he said in a solemn voice.

I pulled out a chair and sat across from him with the books piled between us.

"I've been going over the books," he said, belaboring the obvious. "And I think some changes have to be made."

"What seems to be the problem? We've made more money in the year that I've been manager than in any other year that you've owned the inn."

"Yes, yes, I can see that."

"I think it's largely due to better advertising and to a steadier handling of the reservations."

Before I'd come on board, Uncle Edward had gone through a number of floating managers who often double booked, failed to schedule staff properly, and done nothing to get the word about the inn out to the public.

"That's true," he admitted.

"So what's the problem?"

"Well, for one thing, Mrs. Hazlet is leaving."

"And that's a real loss, but I'm sure that with some effort we can find someone to fill her shoes," I said, barely able to resist pointing out that her leaving was his fault and not mine.

Uncle Edward sighed. "You know when your mother and I decided to give you the job here, it was because you needed work. And to be honest, you hadn't exactly proven yourself to be a leader in your previous positions. And I'm not sure you've proven that here."

"Well, aside from increasing revenue and upgrading staff, I guess that's true," I added with a touch of sarcasm. "Has anyone complained about my performance?"

"Carole has mentioned a few things."

"Has she mentioned that she wants my job?"

Uncle Edward shifted in his chair. "I have discussed that with her, but I haven't yet made a decision."

I nodded and stood up. "I'm not sure what the point is of this conversation."

"I just wanted you to be aware that there might be a possible change in your situation. You'll always have a job at the inn, of course, but you may not be in charge."

"Well, then you should be aware that if I am demoted, I will look for work elsewhere."

I turned and marched out of the dining room. Uncle Edward called my name, but I kept on going.

Chapter Fourteen

By the time I had cruised through the lobby, studiously ignoring Carole standing behind the registration desk, and settled back into my apartment with Dynamite by my side, I was starting to wonder whether my impulsive declaration of freedom had been a bad idea. Wasn't having a job at the inn better than having no job at all? But the picture of working under Carole with her smug officiousness told me that I just couldn't do it.

"What do you think, Dynamite, does a dog, or a man for that matter, have to cling to some shred of self-respect?"

Dynamite gave a big yawn, which I took to mean that my position was so obviously right that it didn't require a discussion.

Reassured, I got out my script and went over several sections where I felt I could present myself more assertively. I was, after all, supposed to be a world-famous young detective. Not some sorry wimp who managed his uncle's inn for a living because he couldn't get steady work acting in the big city. After a couple of hours, I stopped, deciding I had to save some of the manly intensity for the rehearsal. So I had a light supper and changed into my tuxedo. And when Lexi showed up right on time at six o'clock, I headed out, trying not to think about the fact that this might be my last night as manager of the Fireside Inn.

Everyone was on time and jumpy with nervousness, since we were doing a costume rehearsal of the play all the way through from beginning to end. This was the last time to find out where there might be some glitches. There's an old saying in theater that a bad final rehearsal means a great opening night, but I've never met anyone who actually believed that. We were all hoping that everything would go without a hitch.

The first act went well. That was the one where the audience got to know the minor members of the aristocracy who occupied Dumora House somewhere in the south of England. Gerald and Gloria Simmons were naturals in their roles as the snobbish and boring aristocrats. You might almost have said that they were born to the parts, at least when it came to being boring and snobbish. Chelsea—as their docile, simpering daughter—was also convincing in her role. Rick Owens played the butler with admirable formality and just a hint of roguishness, suggesting he might be more than a menial in a suit. The first act ended with the murder of Lord Gerald, who lay center stage, somehow managing to appear less boring dead than he had in real life.

Since it was only a two-act play, I came on in the second act as the young bright boy from Scotland Yard sent out to solve the murder of a member of the titled gentry. I had a series of interviews with minor characters: the gardener, the cook, the scullery maid, and Lord Gerald's secretary. Along the way, the main female characters, Gloria and Chelsea, both made eyes at me as the handsome young man from London. The playwright obviously felt this would build up some mother/daughter tension.

By gathering clues, using logical deduction, and having a whole lot of luck, I finally came to the correct conclusion that the butler was actually Lord Gerald's long-lost son, presumed dead, and he had murdered his father in order to inherit his house, bank accounts, five horses, and innumerable dogs.

So far so good, but now came the bit of stage business where, after resoundingly accusing the butler of being the killer, I had to confront him as he pulled a gun, which I niftily took away from him as I slapped the cuffs on. Rick had consistently proved awkward by either hanging onto the gun or refusing to perform the balletic turn that allowed me to grab his hands. As a result, I approached him warily. I made my declaration of his guilt, poking him gently in the chest. He pulled the murder weapon from behind his back and partially shielded from the audience by my body, he virtually handed it to me. He then turned just enough so that with a light push on his shoulder, I was able to affix the cuffs. Holding his arm, I then gently led him to the front of the stage and made my portentous announcement to the audience that the butler did it.

Mrs. Federico leapt from her front-row seat and began to applaud. "Very good everyone. Rich and Max, that final seen went very well. Do it that way on opening night, and we'll be a smash. And remember, the theater critic from the Lighthouse Point Sentinel will be in the house on Saturday, so everyone come ready to put on a show."

There was much jabbering on the stage as all the performers congratulated each other and themselves on a job well done.

"Don't get your hopes up, pretty boy," Rick whispered in my ear. "I won't be nearly as cooperative on Saturday as I was tonight. You'll have a real tussle getting those cuffs on me."

"Why would you do that? We'll both end up looking bad."

"It doesn't matter if I look bad. Everyone knows I'm just the manager of a hardware store. Climbing on the stage is enough for me to get approval. No one will blame me for a glitch. You're the one who's supposed to be the professional actor. But when I get done, you'll be better known as a professional buffoon."

Rick sidled away with his patented smirk firmly in place and was soon replaced by Chelsea, who looked up at me with something close to adoration.

"You were magnificent tonight," she said. "It was a glorious moment in theater."

"Well . . ." I didn't know quite how to respond to that. Neither *The Butler Did It!* or my performance seemed to me to merit such high praise.

"There will be a cast party on Saturday night after the performance, as you know. I was wondering, sir, if you would care to escort me there . . . and home?" she asked, apparently still in her role as a young lady of leisure.

"I'd be very pleased," I said, glancing over her shoulder to where Rick was glaring at us.

She gave my arm a firm squeeze and flashed a promising smile before she disappeared off into the wings.

I stood there for a long moment staring out at the house and imagining it filled with people. Such a thought was usually capable of filling me with dread, but tonight more important matters were weighing on my mind. I had a young woman whom I had to protect from a professional assassin, an uncle who seemed intent on forcing me onto the unemployment line, and a fellow thespian who was willing to sabotage the entire production just to make me look bad.

An advantage of having multiple problems is that you tend not to dwell on any one of them, I thought as I made my way back to the Fireside Inn.

Chapter Fifteen

The next morning, I took Dynamite out for an early walk and, as casually as I could, made my way up the stairs to the apartment over the garage. I knocked gently on the door, hoping Rachel was awake and would hear me. The door opened quickly.

"Good morning," I said. It never hurts to preserve the niceties.

She just stared, waiting for me to continue.

"There's a bus leaving for New York at one in the afternoon. I'll come by for you at twelve-thirty. We'll take the car. That way you'll be less likely to be spotted." I handed her an envelope filled with money.

She reached out and touched my face. "You're a nice man, Max."

I smiled, not sure whether that comment wasn't damning with faint praise. In my experience, nice wasn't usually what got the girls. You could be nice until the cows came home, and in the end, you still ended up sleeping in the barn.

I went back down the stairs and into my apartment. Dynamite and I had breakfast together. He had dog food, and I had dry toast. His meal looked better than mine, but I wasn't in the mood for a plate of pancakes. We walked out into the lobby in companionable silence. I wondered where I could find a job that would allow me to bring my dog to work. I really didn't like the idea of leaving him alone in a pokey apartment all day.

Dynamite took his place on the pillow beside the fireplace. Today was Mrs. Hazlet's last day, so I went directly into the kitchen before Carole arrived to tell her goodbye.

She looked up from the counter where she was working and smiled.

"I thought you might be in to see me this morning," she said, giving me a tearful smile. "Are you ready for your pancakes?"

"Not this morning, Mrs. H. I'm not really in the mood for food with you leaving."

She came around the counter and gave me a hug. "That's the nicest thing anyone has said to me in a long while." She paused. "Carole was telling me that she expects Edward to make her the inn manager."

"He says he's thinking about it, but I expect he's already decided to go that way."

"Would you stay if that happened?"

I shook my head. "I don't think I could work for her. She's too authoritarian."

"She's a good worker, and smart to boot. But she's a little too full of herself for my taste," she said, returning to her side of the counter and putting out bowls of fruit.

"Where are you going to go?" I asked.

"Don't know just yet. This is Randy's last day here. We're going out to dinner tonight, and I'm half expecting him to suggest that we go back up north together."

I frowned. "I'll miss not having you in town."

"Well, I'm not sure I'll go with him even if he asks. I'm so angry with Edward right now that I can hardly think straight. That's not a good way to be when you're making a major life decision. I think I'll stay around and take some time to think things over. If Randy really cares about me, he'll be patient. What will you do if you leave the inn?"

"I'm not sure. I'd like to stay in Lighthouse Point. Even though I've only lived here a year, it feels like home." I paused. "Do you think it's possible that you and my uncle could get back together?"

"Who knows with Edward? The man hardly knows his own mind, except when it comes to business. If he gives one thought a year to his personal life, it's too much. He acts on impulse."

"Maybe he just needs someone to take him in hand, a sort of assistant who would be in charge of his personal life."

"You mean someone to tell him what to do?"

I nodded. "Not when it comes to business, but everything else."

"Do you think he'd put up with that coming from me?"

"He did return from Florida when he thought you had another guy. That tells you something."

Mrs. H. grunted. "I'll have to give it some consideration."

I went out to the front desk, nodded to Dynamite, who looked up to let me know that he'd spotted me, and I began opening the morning's mail. Uncle Edward walked through the lobby a half hour later, as usual carrying a golf club.

"Max," he said over his shoulder, not stopping, "I'd like to meet with you later on this afternoon. Make yourself available."

I didn't bother to respond since he had already entered the dining room. I greeted the guests who paraded down from their rooms to enjoy the scrumptious breakfast that for many of them was their main reason for staying at the inn. Dynamite got numerous pats on the head, which he accepted as if they were his right. I got smiles, especially from a couple of the younger women, which I suppose I accepted in the same way.

"*Hola*," Gabriella said, coming in the front door. "*¿ cómo estás?*"

"Okay," I said, accustomed to her morning greeting.

"I hear you might be planning to vamoose."

"Where did you hear that?"

"From Carole, *la mujer perra.*"

I didn't know what that meant, but it didn't sound like a compliment.

"You better be careful what you say about her. She may be your next boss."

Gabriella rolled her eyes. "The woman has no sense of humor, and she treats us like *tierra*."

"Would that be dirt?" I asked, taking a wild guess.

"Actually, she treats us worse than that. We're the dirt that dirt is on top of."

"I get your point."

"Can't you talk your uncle into letting you stay in charge? You're not so bad for a boss."

"Thanks for the compliment. Maybe you could write me a nice flowery letter of reference."

"At least you're not stuck on yourself like most other good-looking guys."

"You can put that in the second paragraph of your letter."

Gabriella grinned. "Will do. Is there anything you'd like me to take care of?"

It was so out of character for Gabriella to seek out work that it took a moment for it to sink in.

"Maybe you could check your supply closet and see if there are any cleaning things you need. You can make a report to Carole."

She rolled her eyes, but then nodded happily and headed up the stairs.

I made slow work of the mail since I had very little else to do. Normally, I would have been calling around trying to get a replacement for Mrs. H, but under the circumstances, I figured that could be left to my replacement.

Around noon, Carole came out and took her place beside me behind the reservations desk.

"Mrs. Hazlet has left," she said with no sign of emotion. "I've got a couple of people in mind to replace her. I'll get right on it as soon as I get the go-ahead from Edward."

"Glad to hear that you're on top of things."

She paused, and I thought I might have seen a flicker of emotion cross her face.

"What are you going to do when you leave here?"

"I'm not gone yet."

"Okay. What are you going to do if you leave?"

"Get another job in town."

"Well if you need any contacts . . ."

"That's okay. Gabriella is going to write me a letter of recommendation. That should be enough to land a better job."

"If you're not going to be serious—"

"Right now, I'm going to get some lunch," I said, walking past her and out from behind the counter. I gestured toward Dynamite, who came over to join me. Together, we went into my apartment with our tails held high.

Chapter Sixteen

Once inside my apartment, I took Dynamite out the back way for a quick walk around the garden. After we returned to the apartment, I gave him a treat and filled his bowl with water. I explained to him that I'd be leaving him alone for a while in the afternoon because I had to take Rachel to the bus terminal. I promised that I would be back in time for a longer walk in the afternoon. He seemed to find that acceptable and settled down on his bedroom cushion.

I walked out into the back garden and glanced all around me to make certain that no one was about. Not seeing a soul, I hurried across to the garage and up the stairs to the apartment. I knocked on the door. After several moments, the door opened. Rachel stood there with a sickly smile on her face, then she stepped aside and Brianna took her place, pointing a gun at me. Again, it was deadly looking with a suppressor on the end. The random thought crossed my mind that she must travel with an extraordinary amount of equipment to be able to resupply so quickly.

"Hello, Max," Brianna said. "Don't bother to come inside. We won't be staying."

"Where are we going?" I asked.

"Over to the dining room," she said, pushing Rachel in front of her.

"Why there?"

"You're remarkably curious for someone facing a gun."

"I'm just surprised that *La Loba* takes orders from anyone."

She smiled. "So you know who I am. I guess that doesn't really matter now. Let's just say that the dining room is where my employer wants you to meet your end."

We marched down the stairway with me in the lead, followed by Rachel, and then Brianna.

"The police know all about you. You'll never get away with it," I said, trying to sound convincing.

"The police on three continents know about me, and yet I'm still here, free to roam wild."

I looked around as we headed across the garden. On the one hand, I wished someone would go past and see us, but on the other, I knew that one silent shot from Brianna's gun would put an end to any attempt at a rescue. We went past the door to my apartment and headed to the back door to the kitchen. Fortunately, Mrs. H was gone for the day. I knew that Carole always closed the doors between the lobby and the dining room, so no guests would be likely to wander in on us and become unwitting victims.

Brianna ordered us to move midway into the dining room. As we walked across the room, darkened by mid-afternoon shadows, I snatched a saltshaker off one of the tables and clutched it in my hand. Then Rachel and I took our places next to each other in the center of the room looking at Brianna, who stood there as if trying to decide which of us to shoot first. I'd had some of the happiest culinary experiences of my life in this room eating Mrs. H's breakfasts. It made me sad to think that was all over. After a moment, I realized that Brianna was waiting for someone. I knew that the arrival of her visitor might give me my only opportunity to act.

The door into the kitchen opened, and a man came into the room. From the distance and in the semi-darkness, I couldn't make out his features. He came forward slowly as if he didn't want to disturb Brianna. But as he drew closer, he stepped on a loose floorboard; the inn is full of them. The loud creak caused Brianna to turn her head partway in his direction.

Toward the end of my career on off-off Broadway, I'd starred in *Two Strikes You're Out*, a play about a lad from Iowa who is a pitching phenomenon. He gets drafted by a New York team and comes to the big city where he is quickly debauched by the sins of city life, although all I can remember him ever doing is having a beer and kissing a young woman who didn't happen to be his girlfriend back home. I guess those were the two strikes because horrified by his behavior, he ran back home to the arms of his girlfriend and his job working in his father's feed store, thankful to have kept his purity intact.

The plot was infinitely depressing, but I had a scene where I actually had to pitch onstage. So my role demanded that I learn enough about pitching on a professional level that I appear convincing. I spent many hours at a city park with a former Yankees pitching coach getting the mechanics down. He was very impressed with me by the end. He suggested that with my size and the strength of my arm, I could, with further training, get a spot on a farm team. Being a professional athlete was lower in my estimation than working as a manager in a shore-side inn, so I never followed up on it. Now I hoped I still had the skills.

Just as Brianna turned to look behind her, I went into my windup. And before she could turn back to fire a shot, I threw a hard, fast saltshaker straight down the middle and hit her solidly in the side of the head. The gun fell from her hand, and she dropped to one knee, clearly stunned. The man in the shadows behind her hurried forward, and I recognized Randy Fuller.

"She's a killer, Mr. Fuller. Pick up the gun," I shouted.

He nodded and took up the gun. With no wasted motion, he put a bullet into Brianna's head, and she silently slumped the rest of the way down to the floor.

Rachel gave a brief, stifled scream.

"Shut up," Fuller demanded, pointing the gun at her.

"What are you doing, Fuller?" I said.

"His name isn't Fuller," Rachel said. "That's Sidney Chase, my former boss. The man who's looking for me."

"And thank you both for being so cooperative. You in particular, Max." He took another gun out of his pocket and waved it at us. "I brought this with me because I wasn't sure how I was going to get the drop on *La Loba*, but you made it easy for me."

"Why did you kill her?" I asked.

"She knew that I had hired her, so if she were ever caught, I figured she'd tell all she knew for a lighter sentence. I couldn't have that. Now all the police will find are three dead bodies, all killed with the same gun that most likely can't be traced. No one will ever suspect me, and Rachel won't be able to give evidence that I murdered my partner. A very neat resolution."

I had to admit that I'd been in a lot of plays that had sloppier endings, most of them in fact.

"What about Mrs. H?" I had to ask.

"A wonderful woman and a great cook. I'm sorry to have strung her along, but she really was just my excuse to stay here and observe. I suspected that once *La Loba* put you on the case, Rachel would eventually turn up here. When I saw you coming down from the garage apartment the other morning, I knew where to tell my assassin to go." He paused and nodded. "You really are quite a good detective, Max. It's too bad you'll never appear in that play tomorrow night. But I suppose every cloud has a silver lining. Now your understudy will have a chance to shine."

Rick was my understudy. I cursed to myself. Dying was bad enough but giving him a juicy role was truly aggravating. While Fuller had been doing all that talking, the door to the kitchen had opened again, and another man had entered the room. I tried to look everywhere but at the new guy on the scene because I didn't want to give him away. He moved carefully and seemed to know where all the loose floorboards were.

"So what now, Randy?" I asked to distract him. "You're still short one partner. Won't folks wonder where he went?"

"Oh, that's easy. I'll say he went on vacation. In my line of business, people are used to sudden, permanent departures. And now is the time for yours," he announced, raising the gun.

With a short leap, the man behind him moved forward quickly and brought something down hard on Fuller's shoulder. There was the sound of cracking bone, and Fuller fell to the floor where he lay groaning. My Uncle Edward came forward, looking ruefully at his bent five iron. He picked up the gun.

"Why are you here, Uncle?" I asked.

It was a stupidly irrelevant question, but at that moment, I wanted to know how my life had come to be saved.

"I was inspecting the back garden and decided to come in through the kitchen. A lucky thing, I suppose. And who is this felon?" he asked, giving Fuller a sharp kick in the side.

"Randy Fuller," I said.

"Emily's boyfriend?"

I nodded.

Uncle Edward began to laugh in a way that I hadn't seen in a long time.

Chapter Seventeen

"So you were hiding Rachel McCoy in an apartment over the garage?" Sergeant Azure Blue asked, giving me a stern look, similar to the one I frequently received from Mrs. Federico.

We were seated at a dining room table at the inn forty minutes or so after the police had arrived at the scene. Brianna's body had been removed, and Chase had been taken away: first to the hospital to be treated, then to be arrested. Uncle Edward and Rachel were waiting in the lobby for their turn to be questioned. The fact that I was the first to be interrogated didn't make me feel good.

"That's correct," I said, not even daring to smile in case it were misinterpreted to mean that I found something humorous in my illegal behavior.

"Why didn't you contact us when she came to you?" her beautiful brown eyes were hard.

"Well, I didn't think she would be safe."

"You didn't think we could protect her?"

"To be honest, I didn't. I figured that *La Loba* would be watching the station in case Rachel went there for help. I thought that as a professional assassin, she was perfectly capable of walking into the station and killing everyone there just to get at Rachel. I decided that the only way for Rachel to be safe was to hide her where no one would guess to look for her."

"But you didn't count on Chase masquerading as a guest."

"No, I missed that one."

Blue sighed. "But in the end, you managed to pull off a rescue with a little help from your Uncle Edward."

"I didn't plan quite such a dramatic ending."

"I would hope not."

I paused and took a deep breath. "Am I in trouble?"

"You mean for hiding a person of interest in a police inquiry and concealing evidence?" the sergeant asked. "Why would you think that?"

I detected sarcasm.

"Would it help if I apologized?" I asked.

"Not legally, but a personal apology to me might be nice. I guess I thought we had become friends."

I cleared my throat. "Azure, I am very sorry that I didn't take you into my confidence. I see now that if I had discussed this with you, we would have been able to reach an accommodation that would have kept Rachel safe and not impeded a police inquiry. I was very wrong."

She waved a dismissive hand. "Don't lay it on too thick. It might become unbelievable. I might even come to think that you would do exactly the same thing in the future if the circumstances were the same."

I hung my head and tried to appear contrite. I had a lot of experience with this from my performance in *The Assiduous Adulterer* where I played a young husband who is unfaithful to his wife with three different women. An act was devoted to each tryst. In the final scene, he confesses to his wife and is so sincere and humble that she happily takes him back. It must not have been a very convincing scene because it's the only show I've been in where, when the playwright was introduced at the end, the audience, particularly the women, booed and tried to throw their playbills at the stage. There was even an angry rush by some outraged females in the front of the audience to reach the hapless writer. Fortunately, the director had anticipated the possibility of such a reaction, so a police presence was available and they eventually quelled the crowd. As far as I know, no arrests were made, but the playwright went into an extended period of therapy.

"So are you going to arrest me?" I asked weakly.

She sighed. "One side of me would very much like to do just that. But it hasn't been proved that incarceration does anything to cure stupidity. And, since the end result is satisfactory, I think we can just let the matter rest."

"Thank you," I said, feeling the tension drain from my body. "What's going to happen to Rachel?"

"We're transporting her back to Brooklyn. She'll be the key witness in the trial of Chase for the murder of his partner."

"What about his killing of *La Loba*?"

"That's a tougher one. After all, he did save Rachel's life and yours."

"But his real intention was to cover up for himself. Doesn't *La Loba's* death count for anything?"

"She'd killed countless people in her lifetime."

"Still, she deserves justice."

For the first time, Sergeant Blue smiled. "You have a keen sense of right and wrong, Max. That's one of the things I like about you. To be honest, I don't know how her death will be handled. That will be up to the Brooklyn D.A."

She gave me a nod to indicate that our interview was over. "Would you send in your Uncle Edward?"

I stood up. "Will you still be coming to my play tomorrow night?"

She didn't look up from the papers she was studying. "It all depends on whether I have this case wrapped up by then."

I went out into the lobby where Uncle Edward was talking with Rachel.

"Sergeant Blue would like to see you now, Uncle."

He stood up. It was the first time since his return that I had seen him without his golf club. The police had taken it into evidence. He checked his watch.

"I think we'll have to postpone our conversation until tomorrow morning, Max. How about we meet in the dining room at eleven o'clock?"

"Fine with me." I didn't mind continuing to have a job for another day.

I went back behind the reservations desk. Carol gave me a gimlet eye as I came over to stand next to her.

"This isn't going to help business, you know. Are you trying to sabotage me?"

"You've got it. I almost got myself killed twice just to disrupt your career. Making you miserable is my life's goal."

She began to open her mouth. "Why don't you just go home, Carole? I'll take over here," I said.

"That's the last order you're ever going to give me," she said, moving from behind the desk and striding off across the lobby, her heels clicking angrily on the wood floor.

Maybe so, I thought to myself.

Uncle Edward came out of the dining room a few minutes later and went out through the front door. Probably he wanted to have a rejuvenating walk around town. Rachel was the next to be taken in for questioning. I busied myself behind the desk looking through the classifieds section of the *Sentinel,* figuring I might as well get a head start on my job search. Then I remembered that I had left Dynamite back in my apartment. Deciding the desk could take care of itself for a while, I went into my bedroom where he greeted me by jumping off his pillow and wagging his tail frantically as if he knew that he had been close to becoming an orphan once again.

I gave him a thorough petting, and we took a nice slow walk around the back garden. As we stood there, I thought about the last time I'd been through the garden, a little over an hour ago, and how close I had come to death. I suddenly began to shake. I'd come near death on the stage several times and had even done a couple of dramatic death scenes, one that went on so long that a critic said, "At the end, we were rooting for him to die!" But there was a difference between dying onstage and in real life. Dying in real life would truly be your final performance.

When Dynamite and I finally returned to the lobby, Rachel and Sergeant Blue had just entered the lobby. The sergeant pointed to a uniformed officer by the door.

"He'll go with you to pick up your things from the apartment and then transport you back to the police station in Brooklyn. I'll be emailing them a record of our conversation." Blue put out her hand. "Good luck to you."

Rachel shook her hand and turned toward me. "May I speak with Max for a moment?"

Blue nodded.

Rachel walked over to the desk. "Thank you for everything you did, Max. You're not just a nice guy. You're a real hero." We simultaneously leaned over the desk toward each other, and she gave me a soft kiss on the cheek. She then turned and followed the officer out the front door.

Azure Blue stood by the front door as if uncertain whether to approach the desk. She gave me a long look that I couldn't interpret, and then she too turned and left.

When Uncle Edward returned from his walk some time later, a thought occurred to me.

"Should I cancel breakfast for tomorrow?" I asked.

"No, Carole will take care of it," he said shortly.

I nodded, figuring that indicated my time as manager of the Fireside Inn had come to a close. Time to lower the curtain, send the audience home, and sweep out the aisles.

Chapter Eighteen

The next morning, I had breakfast in my room. I had no desire to eat in the kitchen with Carole ruling the roost. Dynamite and I, after our morning walk, had our breakfasts together. His was rather hardy, mine somewhat more modest due to a lack of breakfast food and the fact that I never liked to eat very much on the day a show opened. I wasn't prone to opening night nausea, as so many actors were, but I didn't want to push my luck.

Dynamite and I positioned ourselves at our usual locations in the lobby. I greeted the guests as they processed in to breakfast, and generally felt as if I were in a state of limbo, waiting for my meeting with Uncle Edward. He did march through the lobby for breakfast, a new, unbent golf club in his hand. He nodded in greeting but didn't share any information by word or gesture about his decision.

The mail arrived and I dutifully thumbed through it. I took a large number of reservations by phone or email. The season was starting to heat up, and soon the desk would become a beehive of activity. The rhythm of commercial life for an inn at Lighthouse Point consisted of two months of increasing work in early spring, culminating in the frantic labors of June, July, and August, to be followed by a gradual decline in the fall and eventually cessation in January, February, and March when the arrival of a guest was like the spotting of a species believed to be extinct. I hoped Carole was prepared to jump into the middle of the rushing torrent.

Finally, my uncle returned to the lobby, right at eleven o'clock, and motioned for me to join him in the dining room. I sat down next to him at a round table. He placed his golf club on the table in front of him like it was a friend he didn't wish to be separated from.

"Okay, Max," he began. "I've been giving considerable thought to this situation, and I've come to several conclusions. First of all, you will keep your job as manager of the inn."

"What about Carole?" I asked.

"She is going to be put in a new position as manager of the kitchen. I am creating two separate entities: the hotel and the restaurant. You will be in charge of the hotel, and Carole will be in charge of the restaurant. There will be separate budgets and a separate chain of command. If all goes well, we may expand the restaurant offerings to include both lunch and dinner. Carole has plans."

I bet she does, I thought.

"And what about Mrs. Hazlet? Will she return to work here?"

"No. She will be coming with me when I return to Florida next week." Uncle Edward cleared his throat. "We will be working out an arrangement in shared accommodations."

"I see. So who will actually be cooking?"

"Carole, for the time being. But she will soon be hiring staff."

"So I will need to hire someone to share my desk duties?"

"Yes. The choice will be yours. Is all of this acceptable to you?" he asked, getting ready to stand up.

"No."

Looking surprised, he settled back down in his chair.

"First of all, why did you change your mind about replacing me as manager."

"I had a lengthy conversation with that young woman, Rachel. When she told me how you had handled her situation, I realized that you are more of a leader than I ever would have expected." He frowned. "I decided that I might have misjudged you. Underneath your mild exterior, there may be more iron than I had expected."

"Okay. Secondly, I am not interested in the job unless I have a five-year contract guaranteeing my employment as long as revenues stay at or exceed the current levels."

To my surprise, Uncle Edward smiled. "Very well. I'll have it drawn up by my lawyer in town. We can sign it before I leave. I see that I did underestimate you. Now, is everything satisfactory?"

I nodded. We stood up and shook hands. Grabbing his golf club, Uncle Edward exited the room.

When I got out in the lobby, Gabriella was just completing her cleaning for the day and was about to leave.

"Gabriella," I said.

"*¿ Que pasa?*"

"How would you like to work here full time for the season?"

"Really!" she said, lapsing into English.

"After you do your clearing, you can take over the desk for the afternoon. You'll even get a 15 percent increase in your hourly wage."

She eyed me suspiciously. "Will I be working for you or for that *perra*?"

"I'm going to continue to manage the hotel."

She grinned. "That sounds great."

"Wonderful. You can start tomorrow. I would suggest that you bring your own lunch because Carole will be in charge of the restaurant."

She rolled her eyes. "I'll bring something I can eat at the desk."

After she left, I walked over to where Dynamite was relaxing on his cushion by the fireplace.

"It all went well, my friend. The most important lesson in life is that you have to put on a good act. You can't let the bastards see you sweat."

Dynamite looked up at me as if to say that, having fur, he didn't share my particular problem.

Chapter Nineteen

I took a quick peek out around the curtain and saw that the house was full. That only meant an audience of a little over a hundred, but it was still a good sign. Back in the dressing room, everyone was a bit nervous except for the Simmonses, who looked as bored as always. I was convinced they would meet their maker with an expression that said, "Is this all there is?"

Chelsea walked past me backstage.

"Are we still on that I'll escort you to the party tonight?" I asked.

"Of course," she replied. "I'm looking forward to it."

We all spent several more minutes getting keyed up—certain that we'd forget our lines—when finally, as it always does, the curtain rose. The first act went by with very few glitches, and most of the second act passed with me giving a fine performance, if I do say so myself. But eventually, we came to the end of the play when I suspected that Rick was going to keep his promise of making me look like a fool. My suspicions were confirmed because as I approached him, ready to make my grand accusation, his face curved into a truly malicious smirk.

I drew close to him, ready to touch his chest and declare that he was the murderer. When I was arm's length away, I recalled my role in *Kung Fu, The Love Story* where I'd played a Kung Fu practitioner who travels to Asia to compete, falls in love with a beautiful Asian girl, and then abandons her to return home to his wife. It was a bit like *Madame Butterfly* with a lot of kicking. One thing I had learned from my training for the part is that two stiffened fingers thrust into the proper location in the solar plexus can virtually paralyze the lungs.

"You are the murderer!" I shouted as loudly as I could. I was facing away from the audience, so I had to use force to project to the back row. Of course, there were only ten rows, but still.

At the same time as I shouted, I thrust my stiffened index finger and middle finger as hard as I could into the lower middle of Rick's chest. The smirk disappeared, replaced by a dazed expression as I watched him struggle, gasping to take in air. I easily spun him around and pulled the gun from the back of his waistband, holding it high in the air to show the audience that I had disarmed the desperado. As he began to collapse forward, close to fainting, I slapped a pair of cuffs on his wrists, making them as tight as I could, like I was the kind of cop who scoffed at the Miranda warning.

I heard him finally take in a shallow breath, which was good because I didn't want him to collapse onstage. Holding on to the cuffs, I dragged him upstage, hearing him making soft whimpering sounds. I stood there for a second to let the silence increase the impact of my words and then I smiled confidently at the audience.

"As you can see," I said, with authority dripping from my voice, "this time, the butler really did do it."

The front rows jumped to their feet and began to applaud. As I stood there absorbing the adulation, next to a still gasping Rick, I knew in my heart of hearts that this is what the theater was all about.

The curtain came down, but it would go up again in a second as the entire cast came onstage.

"Take these damned cuffs off me," Rick demanded hoarsely.

I pretended to search my pockets. "Gee, I seem to have left the key to the cuffs on the prop table."

Before Rick could say more, the curtain went up on the entire cast, and he had to bow with his hands fastened behind his back, looking for all the world in his butler's uniform like a petty aristocrat about to submit to the guillotine.

After three more curtain calls, we had mercy on the audience and let them go. I walked away from Rick who was complaining to Chelsea about his mistreatment. As I headed toward the dressing room, I causally took the key to the cuffs from my pocket and tossed it on the props table.

Chapter Twenty

I changed out of my tux and into more casual clothes in the men's bathroom. When I came out, Mrs. Federico was just walking down the hall. She stopped and gave me an admiring glance.

"That was a spectacular performance. I can see that you are truly a professional." She paused. "The last scene was perhaps a bit more vigorous than it needed to be, but I understand why you improvised." She flashed me a glance that told me she was more aware of the situation than I had realized. "I was very pleased to see that you have . . . well . . ."

"Grown a pair."

She smiled in a vague way and drifted off.

I stopped into the dressing room and sought out Chelsea who was busy examining Rick's wrists. He was obviously still whining about ill treatment at my hands.

"Are you ready to go to the party?" I asked.

"I won't be going with you," she replied. "Rick and I have to stop off at the drugstore to get some crème for his chaffed wrists. You were much too rough with him."

Rick started to smirk, but seeing my stiffened index finger point at him, his expression turned more to fear.

"Okay, well maybe I'll see you there."

I walked out of the dressing room thinking to myself that I'd never understand women. Some of them want you to grow a pair while others would prefer that you never did. I wondered if I should go find Mrs. Federico and see if she needed an escort. Deciding that wouldn't be quite appropriate, I went outside, letting the church door close noisily behind me. I headed down the walk to the street, not certain whether I really wanted to go to the party or not. It would be odd for the leading man not to show up, but the idea of a celebration had lost much of its appeal for me. Plus, my moment of joy had come on the stage; any praise afterward would be anticlimactic.

I reached a dark spot by the side of the church.

"Going somewhere, Max?" a voice asked from the shadows.

I spun around, wondering if there was a spare killer that I had overlooked.

Sergeant Azure Blue stepped out of the shadows.

"You did come," I said. "I didn't see you in the audience."

"I sat at the back in case there was an emergency and I had to leave. You make quite the detective onstage as well as in real life," she said, walking toward me. "I was very impressed, as was everyone else."

"Thanks. It did go well. Of course, it was a team effort."

"But you were the quarterback. Don't be modest."

"I'm never modest. I'm an actor."

She smiled. "Are you on your way somewhere?"

I shrugged.

"Isn't there a party afterward for the cast on opening night?"

"Yeah. I was trying to decide whether to go."

"You have to go, it's part of your role. The show is still going on."

I grinned. "I guess you're right. Would you like to come along as my date?"

"How can I resist an offer from the detective who discovered that *The Butler Did It!*"

"How, indeed?" I said doubtfully.

"Don't worry. I'm sure we'll have a good time together. Don't you think so?"

Suddenly, I was channeling Gabriella. "*Absolutamente!*" I replied cheerfully.

Thank you for purchasing *The Pretend Detective.* The next in the series, *The Left-Handed Man,* will be coming out in the very near future. If you would like to be notified when it is available or want to be made aware of special sales and giveaways of my books, please go to my website at www.glenebisch.com[1] and go to the contacts page. If you leave a message there telling me you'd like to be added to my newsletter list and provide me with your email address, I will be happy to have you join my community of readers. You will also find on the website a description of many of my books with an easy link to purchase.

As always, if you enjoyed this book, a review on Amazon is appreciated. Also, please feel free to contact me directly with your comments and suggestions. I will respond.

1. http://www.glenebisch.com

Made in United States
North Haven, CT
07 October 2023